T0146623

Also by Dennis McKay

Novels
Fallow's Field (2007)
Once Upon Wisconsin (2009)
A Boy From Bethesda (2013)
The Shaman and the Stranger (2015)
The Accidental Philanderer (2015)
A Girl From Bethesda (2017)
Summer of Tess (2018)

Nonfiction
Terrapin Tales, with coauthor Scott McBrien (2016)

BETHANY BLUE

DENNIS MCKAY

iUniverse®

BETHANY BLUE

iUniverse books may be ordered through booksellers or by contacting:

iUniverse
1663 Liberty Drive
Bloomington, IN 47403
www.iuniverse.com
1-800-Authors (1-800-288-4677)

ISBN: 978-1-5320-6555-2 (sc)
ISBN: 978-1-5320-6556-9 (e)

Library of Congress Control Number: 2018915119

Print information available on the last page.

iUniverse rev. date: 01/26/2019

Minor alterations in the establishment of places
were made as the story dictated.

Hazing, gazing creature of the sky,
The cloud it rambles within her eye.
Floating lazily across the celestial dome,
She intuits chaos transposing the Known.

SUMMERTIME 1977

"Sometimes the sky is so beautifully blue it makes me so happy to be alive. Do you know what I mean?" Terri asked Veronica.

Terri leaned back in the lifeguard chair and looked down at her friend, who was cleaning up debris on the pool deck from the previous night's storm. Veronica stuffed a thin branch with spindly green leaves still intact into a rubber trash can. She scanned the pool as children perched on the copingstones. With their toes dangling above the water surface, they anxiously eyed the wall clock at the clubhouse, waiting for the adult swim to end.

"I like the sky when the sun begins to sink and it turns all different shades of heart-crushing purple as though the end of the world were near. Savor it while you can." She looked up. A singular cumulus cloud was lollygagging in an azure sky. "That kinda blue gives me hope, which is always dicey," she said in a tone indicating no further discussion needed.

Checking the time—ten forty-four and forty-five seconds—Terri lifted her whistle to her mouth and fixed a look on the kids leaning over the edge of the pool, as though daring their bodies to take a premature plunge. She took a deep breath, held it for a moment until the second hand struck twelve, and blew on her whistle—*preeeeeeet!*—and all was right in

1

the world of preadolescence as the children splashed into the water, within seconds shrieking "Mar ... co ... Po ... lo!"

This was Terri Landers's second season lifeguarding at the back pool in Bethany West, a neighborhood of more than five hundred modest homes, a ten-minute bike ride from the Bethany Beach boardwalk and the Atlantic Ocean. It was an ideal job at the larger of the two community pools, one block over from the house her parents were renting for the second summer in a row. What more could a twenty-year-old college girl want?

Terri let out a short, sharp *preeeeeeet* on her whistle and yelled, "No running!" to two boys scooting along on the pool deck.

They slowed to a hurried walk before both dived into the deep well. It was the tail end of June, and the summer season was about to crank up big-time.

Nine months a year, Bethany Beach, Delaware, was a sleepy little resort town, but come summer—and especially from the week of the Fourth of July to Labor Day weekend—it was a ruckus of tourists of all ages and sizes, predominantly white. Rarely did Terri see a person of color. There was a long and strong Catholic influence resulting in the establishment, years back, of the Parish of St. Ann Church, which was across Garfield Parkway from the main entrance to Bethany West.

At eleven o'clock, Veronica relieved Terri from the guard chair. A smattering of leaves, all floating on the surface of the pool, was all that remained from last night's storm. The source of the arboreal debris was a stand of trees situated between the pool and a pond that was connected by a shallow channel to the Assawoman Canal.

"Immigrants dug out the canal in the 1890s with picks and shovels," Greg—pool manager, head guard, and local boy—had told Terri a few weeks back when she had asked when it was built. "Makes our light duties seem recreational," Greg added.

And in a way it was recreational, Terri thought as she leaned over the shallow end and scooped leaves from the water with a leaf skimmer, a net attached to a long pole.

After collecting the last of the leaves, Terri retrieved a child's plastic sand pail and a sponge from the storage closet in the clubhouse. She splashed in a couple of squirts of dish soap and filled the pail with warm water from one of the two shower stalls in the women's room. She then entered the pool via the steps at the shallow end.

She stood waist deep in the water, scrubbing the tiles below the copingstones, sliding toward the deep end until she could no longer keep her head above water. Gripping a copingstone, she continued the cleaning process: scrubbing, rinsing the sponge in the pail resting on the copingstone, moving the pail, and moving herself forward to work her way around the pool.

It was a monotonous task, but Greg was a stickler for a clean pool. "Left unchecked, algae can produce dangerous toxins," he had said at the first and only guard meeting in the conference room of the clubhouse, a half hour prior to opening the pool for the season. "We must be vigilant in maintaining a clean and safe environment, from the bathrooms to the pool deck and"—Greg raised a cautionary finger—"maintaining proper pH and chlorine levels in the pool."

Terri did stay vigilant when in the guard chair with her eyes peeled for any sort of trouble in or out of the pool. Even when scrubbing tiles, she kept a watchful eye on the tireless clusters of children bobbing in place while chattering rapid-fire over one another or racing from one pool end to the other.

Parents, sitting in lounge and deck chairs, also kept a watchful eye.

"Timmy, I told you to wait thirty minutes after lunch before going back in," one mother said, motioning for her son to exit the pool.

"*Mo-o-om*." Timmy hollered. "I'm fine."

His mother walked up to the pool edge and index-fingered him out of the water.

Typical day at the pool, Terri thought as she exited the shallow end. On the way to the clubhouse to return the bucket and sponge, her mind drifted to the hubbub of the upcoming weekend. And with Matt, a Bethany Beach ocean guard, whom her mother described as "dangerously handsome," wanting to take their relationship to a more "personal place," it could get very interesting this upcoming Fourth of July weekend.

At twelve thirty, Veronica and Terri headed over to the guard room, a tight space in the clubhouse with a table built into the wall, two folding chairs, and a metal cabinet storing a first aid kit, pool water test kits, Greg's paperwork, and odds and ends. And in a corner was a canvas metal-framed basket for lost and found. Whenever the schedule allowed, Terri and Veronica ate together.

They were sitting at the desk, each at a corner, facing the other. Veronica dug into her brown bag and removed from a plastic baggie half her diagonally cut peanut butter and jelly on rye bread.

"What I have is yours," she said as she leaned forward in her chair and handed the sandwich to Terri, "and what you have is … Well, girlfriend, what's my mystery meat today?"

This was a routine they had established last week. Veronica would bring peanut butter and jelly; Terri would pack a cheese-and-lunch-meat sandwich. Terri handed her newest entry to Veronica, who nearly gagged upon closer inspection.

"Oh my God. That is the most disgusting thing," Veronica said with a turning of her head as she handed the sandwich back to Terri.

"Gretchen … Veronica … Clausen," Terri said, drawing out her full name. "Not liking liverwurst. What would your ancestors from Deutschland have said?"

Terri handed back the peanut butter and jelly. "Next thing, you'll tell me you don't like sauerkraut."

Veronica made a face. *That too.*

She added, "You know I hate that name."

"Ever since we met in seventh-grade homeroom at North Bethesda," Terri said.

"I think fate played a hand in that." Veronica stripped a length of crust off her sandwich.

"In you changing your name to Veronica?"

"No. Remember our homeroom was for *K* through *L*." Veronica continued peeling the crust, disposing of it in her lunch bag. "A secretary in the administration office at North Bethesda mistyped my name—with a *K* instead of a *C*."

"And if not for the transposing of letters, I might not have joined the swim team at Kenwood," Terri said, referring to Kenwood Country Club back home in Bethesda, Maryland.

Veronica made a face. *What do you mean?*

"Because if you hadn't been in my homeroom, maybe"—she paused as though considering it possible—"we wouldn't have become friends and I might have continued swimming for Tilden Woods."

Terri took a bite of her liverwurst-and-swiss-cheese sandwich with mustard on white bread, cut straight down the middle. She held up the sandwich, making a smiley face as though to say, *See, it is yummy.*

Veronica lifted a skeptical brow in regard to the liverwurst. "And after swimming competitively all those years together, on the spur of the moment, we signed up for lifeguard and CPR classes at the Y, not knowing the other had done so." She took a bite of her crustless sandwich, oozing a splotch of peanut butter dangling precariously over the edge that she swiped with her thumb, licking it.

Veronica made a yummy face at Terri, her grinning eyes squinting, *Back at you.*

"Then we both end up with summer jobs as guards at the same pool in Bethany Beach no less." She lifted her brow again but this time in a knowing manner. "Fate," she said in a tone indicating, *Case closed.*

Terri did wonder, though, if they would have become friends even without fate playing a hand. Veronica, the most formidable, desirable of girls, had a sharp wit, a nose for phoniness that she would immediately call out, and an attitude of one who didn't care whether she was liked.

Her attitude proclaimed, "This is who I am. Take it or leave it."

From the start, Terri had found Veronica intriguingly different, someone she would have most likely gravitated toward for friendship over the course of their junior high years, same homeroom or not.

Veronica asked, "Any plans for this evening?"

"Going to the drive-in movie in Ocean City with Matt."

"Remember rule number one," Veronica said with meaning. "Protect the fortress."

Terri's dad wasn't coming down until later in the week, so she and her mom ate dinner together.

Her mother inquired, "What are your plans for the evening?"

"Going to a movie with Matt." Terri looked up at her mother sitting across the Formica dinner table from her.

Her mother speared her fork into a stack of string beans on her plate.

Then she paused with the fork lifted. "That drive-in in Ocean City?" Her bloodhound instincts were on full alert.

Terri stopped cutting into a tender chicken breast and looked up, her expression pained. "Yes, *Mo-o-om.*"

After helping her mother with the dishes, Terri went to her bedroom to get ready for her date with Matt. As usual, she decided to keep it casual: T-shirt, jean shorts, and flip-flops. She looked in the mirror over her dresser. She liked what she saw.

Terri was no longer swimming competitively. She swam through freshman year of college but tired of the early-morning practices. But she still maintained a swimmer's build. Standing five foot eight tall, which she had reached by age thirteen, Terri had been blessed with a well-proportioned physique complemented by substantial yet compactly formed shoulders that gave the impression of feminine power held in reserve. Her strong, trim arms and legs had nary an ounce of fat.

In her one-piece swimsuit, the Kenwood swim coach had told her, "Terri, you have the look of the perfect competitive female swimmer."

Included in that look were eyes that shined dark blue and true, set above cheekbones positioned high and tinged with a hint of pink, slanting down to a firm jawline. It was a face that belonged with her body, a perfect match.

Her maternal grandmother told Terri on her thirteenth birthday, "Terri, my dear, you are the epitome of the girl next door."

At the time, Terri had felt conflicted about the designation. It came across as wholesome, yes, but also as unglamorous in her mind. Glamour was what the girls on the cover of *Teen* magazine and Veronica had in spades. They had a certain look of splendid nonchalance that in Terri's thirteen-year-old mind had translated to glamorous.

But now at twenty, she told herself that she was pleased with not only the way she looked but who she was—a smart, attractive college girl with a great summer job in an even greater locale.

By seven thirty, Terri was waiting at the front door. Her mother, mercifully, was on the porch reading the *Washington Post*. Her mother had never been completely sold on Matt, and though she was not unfriendly toward him, there was a certain tension in the air when she was in his presence.

Matt had always been polite—possibly overly so—to Terri's mother, but she had sensed something about him that set off her maternal alarm system. And even when not in his presence, the mention of his name could put Terri's mother on alert—a scrunch of her brow and a squint of the eyes, revealing silent disapproval.

Terri laughed to herself when she replayed in her mind her reaction to her mother's inquiry about the drive-in movie with Matt. "Yes, *Mo-o-om*," she had replied with childish aggravation.

It was the same response little Timmy at the pool had when his mother made him exit the pool. *Mo-o-om.* But her mother's instincts in regard to Matt being not only dangerously handsome but a danger to her only child's virtue had validity.

Never had Terri been so physically attracted to a boy as she was with Matt. And besides his good looks, Matt had an animal magnetism that was hard to resist, an invisible force field of raw, sexual charisma. She wasn't in love with Matt and had always thought that she would save herself for true love, ideally the man she would marry.

But a combination of Bethany Beach's sunny, warm weather, the good-time-let-it-all-hang-out atmosphere of her summertime contemporaries, and a growing desire to share her body with a studly guy had wavered her position. It seemed her corporeal being was in a struggle with her conscience.

The Shore Drive-in was off Route 50, three miles east of Ocean City. Only one car was in line at the ticket booth, a small shack where a girl was selling tickets through a window. The towering projection screen was already showing advertisements for local businesses: Phillips Seafood Restaurant, a car dealership, and a surf shop. After paying at the ticket booth, Matt navigated to the back, parking beside an audio port.

"Popcorn?" Matt asked as he lifted his chin in the direction of the concession stand.

"Sure," Terri replied with a nod.

By the time Matt returned, nightfall was settling over the dirt and gravel parking area, which had a few other cars, all parked discreetly apart. The movie that would be shown was *Cassandra Crossing*, about a deadly virus on a train crossing Europe.

"First of two keggers this week at the guard house tomorrow." Matt grabbed a handful of popcorn. "We're calling it Hump Wednesday."

"Is that a double entendre?" Terri asked as she slanted a look at Matt.

"One meaning," Matt said, "but I am open to your interpretation." He flashed his killer smile at Terri before shoveling the popcorn in his mouth and chomping it down.

"Ha hah," Terri said. "Okay if I ask Veronica?"

"Absolutely," Matt replied. "Can never have enough beautiful girls."

Terri shot a look at Matt, who shrugged and smiled his handsome boys-will-be-boys smile. "And if she has a sister, bring her along too."

"Sorry," Terri said. "Just an older brother."

"He's welcome to come," Matt retorted.

"I'd ask him, but he lives in Colorado." After a pause and a clearing of her throat, Terri inquired, "How was guard duty at the ocean today?"

"Gentle surf, nary a rescue." Matt put his arm around Terri's shoulder.

Whenever they were together alone, Matt had little to say, his mind seemingly on one subject. He had never had a real conversation with her, mostly talking about the social scene in Bethany and his lifeguard buddies.

Matt was immersed in his Bethany Beach orbit, not that Terri didn't realize that she also was in a similar orbit. It just would have been nice if just once Matt had asked about her life at college other than the perfunctory exchange about majors or her interests away from Bethany. Never had he tried to get below the surface to see who was there and what she had to say.

But Matt had plenty to say when the mood struck him during parties at the guard house. He could be Mr. Congeniality: telling silver-tongued jokes with perfect timing, talking to one and all with an exuberant air of one having the time of his life, and listening intently and laughing on cue when others had regaled an old escapade.

At times Terri wondered why Matt had chosen her when he could have had most any girl in Bethany. Was it her prowess as a swimmer that he had witnessed firsthand on guard duty? Or did he like *wholesome* girls? Or was it … who knew what was going on in the mind of a twenty-one-year-old hunky guy. Part of her had been tempted to ask, but she thought better. Veronica would never have considered such a question to a boy.

As "Coming Events" flashed on the big screen, Terri noticed that Matt had not bothered to attach the audio receiver to his driver's window of his big and roomy four-door sedan, a hand-me-down from his father.

With his arm still on her shoulder, Matt brought Terri close, rupturing the cardboard box of popcorn that had been squished between their thighs, spewing popped kernels of corn out of the crushed remains. He then nuzzled his face into her neck, puckering softly at her flesh.

Terri removed the crushed box of popcorn between them and placed it carefully on the floor as Matt's lips found hers. She felt the strong pressure of his tongue on hers and his strong body pressing against her, and his downy-soft scent filled her nostrils. He was very hard to resist as she felt a warm glow of desire flush her face and neck.

Matt leaned back. "Why don't we move to the back where we'd have more room?"

Terri's attention was momentarily diverted as a preview for *The Omen* lit up the screen in a swath of cherry red with a cemetery as a backdrop.

"Whaddaya say?" Matt asked in an encouraging, solicitous tone.

Terri knew she shouldn't, but she was in the moment, a sexual attraction moment where her good senses had deserted her. "Okay," she said in a hurried, panting voice, a tone she did not recognize.

The back seat was spacious, and quickly Matt was on top of Terri with one hand behind her neck and the other under the back of her shirt, his fingers on the bra strap that he uncinched effortlessly. It flashed in Terri's mind that this was not his first flawless uncinching.

Matt slid a hand over the side of her ribcage and caressed one of her breasts and then the other. Terri could feel the heat coursing her body, down her chest, and, oh boy, between her legs. She was in uncharted, dangerous territory.

Matt leaned back to a kneeling position with his legs between hers. He unbuttoned the top button of her jean shorts and then placed his dexterous fingers on each side of her waistband, as Terri lifted her buttocks to assist in the undressing. Her cotton undies were a flimsy guardian of the fortress.

He then tugged his T-shirt out of his shorts and pulled it off in one swift motion. She noticed his golden-skinned torso so finely sculpted. *Was this the moment I would go all the way? Let a guy enter me?*

She had fantasized what it would be like with Matt, a sensation like stars bursting all throughout her body, a rapturous, lustful, let-it-all-out sexual encounter with this young Adonis. Terri was losing herself to the moment.

"I have a rubber," Matt said as his fingers slid along the elastic frontier of her undies.

Something in his voice warned Terri off, breaking the spell as she heard her mother's voice, "Dangerously handsome."

"No, Matt." Terri pushed his hands off her underwear, scrunched up to a sitting position, and brought her knees into her chest.

Tonight the fortress would not be breached.

At the dawn of adulthood
There comes a tapping,
A silent inevitable sapping,
A Changing of the Guard

The following evening after dinner, Terri rode her bike from her house a couple of blocks down Half Moon Circle to Veronica's house at 604 Holly Court. Terri's house was at 604 Juniper Court, and Veronica had said at lunch yesterday that having the same numbers meant Terri's parents were destined to buy their rental.

"My parents purchased last year. This year is your turn where the inevitable meets reality," were Veronica's last words as they had departed the guard room after lunch.

Veronica, who also had gone on a date last night, got called to emergency guard duty at the front pool when she had arrived at work this morning, so they never had a chance to talk, other than Terri telling her about the party at the guard house tonight. Terri was curious to hear how her date went, as she knew Veronica was about Matt and the drive-in.

Terri liked hearing Veronica's take on dating guys, and though she didn't agree with her dispassionate, abrupt manner in breaking up for seemingly no good reason, Veronica possessed a certain feminine understanding of the male mind-set.

From Veronica's house, they rode their bikes into the town of Bethany Beach, a strip of typical beach resort businesses, among which were a miniature golf course, a general store selling anything from sandals to beach chairs and umbrellas, a grocery store, a couple of knickknack and clothing shops, a seafood restaurant, and a submarine shop.

At the end of the strip was the boardwalk, a twelve-foot-wide wooden promenade running parallel to the Atlantic shore with a motel, a few shops, a family restaurant, and a window walk-up selling french fries, burgers, and hot dogs.

After they bought a medium-size bucket of fries, Terri and Veronica took a seat on a boardwalk bench, keeping their backs to the ocean while people watching and snacking. There were families with small children, some pushing baby carriages along the boardwalk, middle-aged couples holding hands as they strolled, and then the older folks sitting on benches taking it all in.

But the hum of energy emitting from the young teens hustling and bustling about brought back memories to Terri of her first time here as a thirteen-year-old girl. It was a world unto itself: the shrieking laughter and voices, the rapid and energized movements of kids darting here and there, a rumor of a party on Fifth Street beach after dark, or who knew what. It was not the events as much as the anticipation in such an invigorating environment that had captured Terri. It was a whole new world.

"They remind me of us at that age." Terri turned her attention to a circle of girls talking and laughing over each other, their sparkling eyes bursting with life as though this very moment was the best moment ever.

"Yeah," Veronica said with a trace of remembrance in her voice.

"I will never forget my first time here." Terri paused momentarily as that indelible memory registered in her mind. "I came down with my parents for a three-day weekend, and we stayed on the second floor with a balcony overlooking the ocean at the Blue Surf." She lifted her chin to the two-story motel anchored on the corner of the strip and the boardwalk, its name in white fonts against sky-blue siding.

"It was the freedom that I remember most," Veronica said.

"I still savor it," Terri replied as she recalled the end of last semester, right through finals.

She would awake each morning in her dorm room, not worried about her next exam but rather anticipating the mingling scent of sea air and french fries that wafted on the boardwalk when the wind was just right. It had been a pleasant, calming way to awake in the morning before the reality of the day came upon her, as she swung out from bed to cram at her desk for another final.

"Shall we wander over in a bit to the keg party at the guard house?" Veronica dipped a tater in a tiny paper cup of ketchup.

"Matt said we're attending the Hump Wednesday kegger."

"Seriously?"

"I called him on it," Terri said, "and he turned it around on me."

"Let me guess." Veronica looked off as though envisioning the exchange. "He had that handsome Matt smirk from ear to ear," she retorted in a teasing tone.

Terri had a sense that Veronica was a tad envious of her dating Matt, while the other stronger part wanted nothing to do with seeing one guy for the entire summer. She fingered two fries, started to dip in the ketchup, which Veronica was offering, and pulled back, making a face indicating, *No thanks.*

"I have just one admirer. You, my dear Veronica, have a whole two-story house of guys chomping at the bit to have their way with you."

"I am saving myself for the man I will marry," Veronica said without a bit of humor.

"Aren't we all?" Terri said.

"No," Veronica said. "We *all* are not. We must keep the fortress secure."

From when first they met in seventh grade to this very moment, Veronica Clausen had been the best-looking girl in not only school but any setting, the reincarnate of Elizabeth Taylor in her youth. She was a raven-haired beauty with full pouty lips, twin rows of perfectly formed teeth, and perfectly flared eyebrows arched over devastating jade-green eyes that could draw in a boy and reduce him to a muttering jumble of words.

Complementing Veronica's beauty was a voluptuous body with generous bulges and nubile curves in all the proper places, which drew the eyes of not only her contemporary males but the fathers at the swimming pool.

The fathers, anywhere from late twenties to early fifties, stole quick yet lingering peeks as Veronica extended her supple arms over the pool edge, her curvaceous torso stretching out and tightening the already tight fit in her swimsuit as she netted leaves from the pool. She was a magnetic force that drew the attention of males of all ages and sizes.

"So what happened at the drive-in last night with Matt?" Veronica asked as they both watched two teenybopper boys sprinting full-bore down the boardwalk neck and neck, their arms swinging wildly back and forth, heading to who knew where.

"The fortress was nearly breached." Terri dipped a fry into the cup of ketchup in Veronica's hand. She went on to give a detailed account of the close encounter.

"I can only imagine how hard Matt is to resist." There was hint of wistfulness in Veronica's voice, as though *possibly* the thought had crossed her mind.

Though Veronica had a self-awareness of her physical attributes, she had never lorded them over Terri or other girls, for that matter. But Terri wondered if she couldn't pull it off without a hitch—steal a boy from an unsuspecting girl with little more than a honed-in look from her intoxicating eyes and a flutter of her long and dark eyelashes.

Terri asked, "How was your date last night with—"

"Fishing boy," Veronica said in regard to the college guy who was working the summer as a deckhand on a deep-sea fishing boat in Ocean City. "Rule number two." Veronica raised her hand as though taking an oath, spreading her index and middle finger in a V shape. "To protect the fortress, prevent the invading male horde from getting to second base."

They exchanged looks for a beat before Terri added, "Go on, Miss Clausen."

"It was our third date, and we were making out on the beach." Veronica shook her head at the memory. "We started out kissing and then lying side by side on a blanket. It was nice, a good-looking, hunky guy under a starlit sky," Veronica said with another more pronounced shake of the head. "Fishing boy placed a hand firmly and aggressively between my legs."

"What were you wearing?" Terri asked.

"My culottes. You know, the pair made of denim. I removed his hand and told him to never do that again."

"And?"

"He was in heavy rut and tried again. I slapped him so hard in the face." Veronica's attention was diverted for a moment by an elderly stooped-shouldered man with sparse white hair and a rickety gait pushing a wheelchair-bound woman of similar age with gray, papery skin and sad eyes.

Veronica then continued, "The nerve. Didn't even bother with second base." She lifted her brow, her eyes smiling benign naughtiness. "Might have let him steal it too." Veronica shrugged as she looked at Terri, a secret smile in the corner of her mouth. "Rule number six. There is an exception to every rule."

Much less offenses could cause Veronica to tire of a boy and abruptly cut things off by not taking phone calls or saying no without explanation to a request to go out. Or when in the company of a rejected boy in a social setting, her expression could range from acting as though they had never gone out to a been-there-done-that look. It was fun while it lasted, so, *No hard feelings. Let us move on and act as though none of it ever happened.*

The most recent shunning of an admirer, which Terri had witnessed earlier in the season on the beach, was with a graduate student, working the summer as a beach boy. He was setting up an umbrella and chairs near where Veronica and Terri were sitting. Veronica had already told him that she didn't want to go out any longer.

After he had set up the umbrella, he maneuvered his way around the crowded beach, approaching Terri and Veronica, who was wearing tortoiseshell sunglasses. Her expression was so utterly blank and indifferent as he stole a crestfallen peek at the beautiful ice maiden.

Terri had asked, "Veronica, why not at least acknowledge him?"

"Because," Veronica said as she removed her sunglasses to apply sunscreen to her face, "when it's over … it's over."

Party hearty to your hearts content
Live for today ...
Until tomorrow is spent

After finishing every last one of their french fries, Terri and Veronica headed over to the guard house, a ramshackle two-story clapboard structure, one block from the boardwalk on Atlantic Avenue, which ran parallel to and a stone's throw from the ocean. Turning the corner on Atlantic, they could hear the rhythmic beat of Credence Clearwater Revival playing "Bad Moon Rising."

At the front door, Veronica gave Terri a look, indicating, *Let the fun begin.* Terri opened the door into the foyer. A piercing bark of laughter drew their attention to the living room on their right.

Lounging on a sofa were three ocean guards wearing T-shirts with their school name emblazoned across the front. One was in cutoffs and barefoot, and the other two were in gym shorts and flip-flops. They were drinking Schlitz "Tall Boys" in sixteen-ounce cans and talking in that spirited jock way, with much animation and pronounced hand gestures to emphasize a point. Their loud voices competed with the thumping beat of the music. There were other guards standing around and of course girls, who either were local or working in Bethany Beach for the summer.

The decor of this rental property was what one would expect for housing a horde of college boys. The living room furniture was Goodwill variety: over-the-hill cushy sofa, lumpy armchairs, and a dinged and dented, yet sturdy, nautical table with two recessed holders on the tabletop, which wrought iron legs supported.

On the living room wall hung the sole contribution from the tenants to the furnishings: a tapestry featuring seven dogs closely gathered around a starkly lit table studying their cards—and each other. At the bottom of the artwork was the title and author, *A Friend in Need* (1903), Cassius M. Coolidge. Terri had previously seen it in the foyer of a fraternity house at college.

She thought this piece of wall art was such a guy thing. And she did not mean it as a compliment—nor, for that matter, in a disparaging way. It just was how she perceived the minds of guys worked … or … did not work.

Adjoining the living room was an empty dining room that flowed into a small kitchen that could be entered through a doorway from the hallway foyer. To the rear of the kitchen was a hallway lined with bedrooms. A staircase in the foyer led to more bedrooms on the second floor, a level Terri had never been on.

The umbrella guy had told Veronica that the second floor was known to some of the guards as the *bang-bang* suites. Veronica had relayed this a while back to Terri during lunch at the swimming pool.

"Boys are such dummies," Veronica asserted with a hint of hostility in her tone. "Once word gets out, what girl in her right mind would do it in a *bang-bang* room?"

The guards, many of them rugby and lacrosse players, were all in excellent shape, having to swim a half mile each morning, plus perform calisthenics, before duty. They were like a team, with team spirit, gregarious and outgoing, who took their summer employment seriously and their social life with carefree vigor.

Their job was essential to not only the well-being of the tourists who swam in the ocean but the tourist industry. A drowned swimmer would not be good for business. A few weeks back, Matt had told Terri that during a turbulent two-day stretch of rip currents he had pulled six people from the water.

"Two boys around twelve, three men, and an elderly woman."

They were on the Bethany boardwalk, leaning on a railing as they watched dusk settle over the ocean in shadowy shades of gray.

"It was exhausting," Matt said with a sigh, "not only the physical exertion but the mental strain of staying vigilant."

Terri and Veronica turned to enter the living room when the hurried creak of footsteps on wooden stairs brought their attention to the stairway, as Matt quick-stepped his way down, stopping on the bottom step in front of Veronica and Terri. Terri got a whiff of English Leather cologne.

"Welcome, ladies," he said in a carefree, let-the-party-begin tone. He was dressed in a pink polo shirt with the collar pulled up, khaki Bermuda shorts, and T-strap sandals.

Matt looked stunningly handsome. His rippled hair of gold, which dangled across his forehead just so, was still damp from the shower, and his golden, chiseled face magnified his light blue eyes. He looked like a catalogue model for beachwear.

There was a half keg in a steel bucket of ice set up in the dining room, and Matt served Terri and Veronica beers in plastic cups. Veronica then wandered off into the living room, drawing the attention of two guards, who were talking her up as though trying to outdo the other, while Veronica listened, smiled, and laughed … all on cue.

Two girls, a brunette and a blonde, who worked on the beach setting up umbrellas came in from the kitchen. Both were fit, pretty, and local. Terri wasn't sure if they attended college or not. She thought, *Maybe a local junior college.*

Matt said hello to them, and both replied in singsongy unison, "*Hell-loo*, Matt." They might as well have let out a cheer, "Matt, Matt, he's our man. If he can't do it, no one can!"

Terri smiled a hello, which was returned before both girls returned their attention back to Matt. She sensed they considered her and Veronica rivals—not so much in anything they said but more a distant look of appraisal every time they crossed paths. It was as though they were sizing up the competition when they offered a throwaway *hi* as they lugged umbrellas and chairs on Third Street beach, where Terri hung out on her off days, which was also Matt's guard station.

The first time Terri had met Matt was when she came in from swimming out past the break. She had swum between two red jetty flags, boundary markers for safe swim areas. Back and forth she went: two strokes and breathe … two strokes and breathe through the undulating current, her body seemingly craving for more until finally she came in more out of boredom than fatigue.

"Impressive," Matt said from the lifeguard chair. He had zinc oxide on his nose and cheeks, highlighting his bronze face. Perched up high, he brought to Terri's mind some Nordic god of sun and surf overseeing his domain.

Terri offered a shy smile. Matt grinned back, his even, white teeth glistening in the bright sunlight. It was a gorgeous and remembering smile.

Keeping his eyes fixed on the ocean, Matt struck up a conversation, asking Terri if she swam competitively and what her events were. He also mentioned that he was on his college diving team. That evening they went out for pizza, and rather seamlessly they began going out.

Though it seemed much longer, Terri had been dating Matt for not quite four weeks. They had never talked about an exclusive relationship, but Terri took it as something understood, but one of the umbrella girls, the blonde, Brittany, was making it very clear to Matt her availability.

"*Ma-a-att*," Brittany said in a cooing, annoying voice, "we're having a beach blast on Fifth Street this Saturday after work. Hope to see you there."

Terri and Matt were standing at the keg, obviously together.

Terri leaned closer to Matt, her eyes saying to Brittany, *He. Is. With. Me.*

Brittany ignored Terri, who was a good four inches taller than this bleached blonde with grungy dark roots exposed, who kept her eyes flirtingly on Matt, batting her false eyelashes at him as though it was just the two of them. *She's good*, Terri thought, *the perfect other woman on a soap opera.*

"Let you know, Brittany." Matt shrugged. "Not sure what's going down this weekend."

What? Terri thought. But she didn't show any emotion, taking a casual sip of her ice-cold beer.

"Good beer, Matt." Terri looked up at him and tried her damndest to act as though Brittany was not in her presence. She took Matt's hand in hers and led him into the living room and away from the competition.

The keg party was a blast with over fifty people filling the house—guards, umbrella staff, and friends of both groups—all immersed in laughter and stirring conversations about life in Bethany.

Matt was standing in the middle of the living room among a circle of partiers, listening, laughing, and adding to the conversation. "Last week, Kirk and I had to break up a fistfight on the beach between two forty-year-old men over a snide comment made to one man's wife."

People began to drift over to the circle drawn by the infectious tone of Matt's voice, one that said, *You don't want to miss this one.*

"While Kirk and I," Matt said with a lift of his chin across the circle toward his fellow guard, "were pulling the flailing, beer-bellied Sir Galahads apart—"

"They looked more like Friar Tucks." Kirk cut in to a ripple of laughter.

More kids drifted over, the circle now three rows deep.

"I stand corrected," Matt said with index finger raised. "While we were pulling apart the two flailing Friar Tucks, the wife was screaming in a Dixie twang," which Matt mimicked. "'Kick his ass, honey bear. Kick it good.'"

The entire party broke up into hooting, hands-on-knees laughter at Matt, the showman.

"What about the time—?" Kirk asked in a tone of one-upmanship. He then told about a gust of wind blowing a rental umbrella into the ocean. "Whizzed right past my ear while on duty in the guard chair, right into the water like a guided missile. We had to close the beach."

"I can see it now, Kirk." Matt grinned. "Eventually your death would have been attributed to a jilted umbrella girl who, rumor had it, threw the javelin in school, and she decided to teach you a lesson you would never forget."

More uproarious laughter emerged from the room, save the brunette umbrella girl who was not laughing, her face a tight-lipped blank. Terri wondered if Kirk and she had been an item at one time and if Kirk had broken it off.

The conversations were never about politics or world events. It was as though they were living in a private world of fun in the sun. These were the last carefree days of childhood before moving on to grown-up life, so party hearty and worry about the real world after graduation.

One divergent conversation that drew an audience was from a couple of surfers regaling about their trip to Australia. Both were tall and lean, one with sandy-blond hair and the other jet-black. Both had wickedly dark tans.

"In Byron Bay, *duuude*," the blond said in his exaggerated surfer-dude dialect of drawing out vowels, "I didn't think I was going to make it out of a drainer. It was sucking *sooo* hard."

Like his surfer bud, the blond dude appeared a few years past college age, most likely dropouts. And beneath the bonhomie was an unfinished quality of adolescence, a pair of Peter Pans on surfboards in search of the perfect wave.

As the night wore on, Brittany and her girlfriend ended up leaving the party with the two surfer dudes. *Good riddance*, Terri thought as she was sitting on the sofa with Matt. People were standing about. The party was one big shout.

Matt noted their departure and then turned his attention to Terri. "How about some quiet time on a blanket on the beach?"

"I've got to be home soon," Terri said.

"Then we have no time to waste," Matt replied, standing and offering his hand to Terri.

Matt unfurled a royal-blue fleece blanket near the shoreline. *Allegheny College* was scrolled in white along the lower right corner. Below the school name was his name, *Matt Meadows.*

"Ladies first." He offered his hand for Terri to sit.

This was her first time on the beach at night with Matt, and she wondered if he had used this blanket with other girls at this very spot. *Was this one of his patented moves?*

But it was nice to be away from the hubbub of the party, with the crashing surf and the silver light of the moon casting its glow across a blue-black ocean. Though Terri told herself that she was not allowing Matt to take things too far. His wishy-washy answer to Brittany about attending the beach blast had set off alarm bells. It was becoming clear that Matt considered their relationship nothing more than a summer fling. *Let's have a good time and then return back to our respective schools and continue on with our lives.*

"Chad and Darren," Matt said in reference to the surfer dudes, "think they have a great life." He looked to his left and then his right as though making sure no one was around to hear what he had to say. "But where are they going to be in five years? Still traveling the globe from beach to beach."

"I wondered the same thing," Terri stated as she saw an opening. "Where do you see yourself in five years?" She turned to Matt, who kept his gaze on the shore as wave after wave pounded the beach.

She wasn't sure why she had asked him this. Maybe it was in retaliation for his wishy-washy answer to Brittany about attending the beach party. Or was she a tad insecure dating Matt?

She held no upper hand with Matt. In fact she felt as though he had control, though she wondered whether he was even aware of any of this. Just breezing through the college years before heading into a successful career in whatever he chose.

"After I get my degree in engineering at Allegheny next year, I would like to work for an established engineering firm for a few years while working toward my master's degree in night school. I'll save my money and then start up a civil engineering company with a couple of buddies back at school."

He inclined his head toward Terri as if to say, *Does that answer your question?*

This was a new version of Matt, one that Terri had not seen. It was a critical Matt, a Matt with a plan for his future without a hint of bonhomie. Of course that wasn't the direction Terri had inquired about, but he had adeptly avoided it with an informative answer.

Matt made a face indicating, *Enough of the serious talk.* He lifted Terri's chin, leaned into her, and kissed her on the lips. He leaned back, his eyes seeking hers.

"This summer is my last hurrah. School is stressful, and after that I have to find a job and get real about my life." He kissed her again, bringing his arm around her waist. The breezy salt air carried his tantalizing scent of masculine youth and aftershave rushing in all around her. In the distance, the faint sound of laughter could be heard before the crashing surf swallowed it up.

Matt whispered in her ear, "I knew when first I saw you swimming in the ocean." His lips grazed her lips, hovering as though waiting for the inevitable.

Terri leaned back from Matt, her eyes now seeking his. He smiled a light airy smile. The old Matt had returned. And in his gaze, she saw attentiveness and a kind of hunger that at this moment she found agreeable. *He wants me.*

Matt's lips landed softly on hers. While holding the kiss, he gently brought her down and lay on top of her, their tongues locked in each other's mouth. Matt brought his hand under Terri's T-shirt and slipped it under her bra. Her carnal side was in full pet, as she felt the heat rise in her chest.

The whine of an automotive engine and the cranking sound of shifting gears accompanied by a dim bar of light entered their space.

"Awg," Matt growled as he rolled off Terri.

Coming from the north end, along the top of the beach, was a pickup truck.

"What is it doing out here?" Terri inquired as she sat up, looking across the beach.

"Beach trash collection." Matt stood and offered his hand to Terri.

The truck came to a stop ten yards away. The shadowy image of the driver got out, silhouetted in the headlights for a moment as he made his way in front of the vehicle to a trash can located at the end of the path leading to the beach. He lifted the can out of its wooden-slatted holder and carried it to the back of the truck, dumping the contents into the bed before returning the trash can.

On his way back to the cab, he slanted a peripheral glance down toward the shoreline as though sensing he was being watched. He stopped momentarily and then veered off toward Terri and Matt. As he neared, Terri heard the faint jingle of a string of keys attached to his belt.

"Beach is closed after dark," he said in a matter-of-fact voice.

His face was that of an adult, maybe forty, but there was something naïvely boyish about his expression as though he had never completely grown up. He was wearing a pair of brown trousers and matching short-sleeved work shirt. A white name patch over his left breast identified him as Kermit, which in Terri's mind fit him perfectly, *Kermit the boy-man.*

"We'll be on our way," Matt said through a rueful grin.

"That'd be best all around," Kermit said with an affirming nod directed at Terri. "Damn near ran over a pair of lovebirds last week." He smiled a gap-toothed grin. "Wouldn't want that on my résumé."

Back in front of the guard house, Terri told Matt she needed to head on home. "Have to get to work early tomorrow to vacuum the pool and clean the skimmers."

But that wasn't the real reason. She didn't want to explain that she had a tacit agreement with her mother to be home by eleven. Terri never wanted to worry her mother, who always waited up for her to come in.

This wouldn't have happened if Terri were a boy. Bethany was ultra safe, but Terri understood. If she had a daughter, she would worry also.

"I thought we might go upstairs to my room?" Matt made a face that said, *What do you think?*

"To your *bang-bang* room?"

Thunder in the morning
Brings fair warning
To all the fair maidens
Beware the Raven
Under the cloak of safe haven

Terri woke to the rumble of thunder, which caused her family beach house—a three-bedroom box with aluminum siding supported by a crawlspace cinderblock foundation—to shudder. Last semester, she had taken a course in earth science and had learned that heat causes the air to expand so rapidly that it generates a shock wave, or thunder.

Terri had always enjoyed the sound of early-morning thunder, but now there was another reason, the chance that the pool would be closed for the day. If so, she would dig into her required summer reading list from school. Terri attended a small liberal arts college in upstate New York. Though the winters were snowy and cold, she didn't mind, enjoying the change of all four seasons. The college had a total of four thousand students and was built in the late nineteenth century. The architecture was basically steeple and stone and brought to mind New England. Actually the school was only fifty miles from the Vermont line.

At school, Terri had an occasional date but nothing serious. She mostly liked to go to parties in a group of guys and girls or with a girlfriend. Her two biggest romances had both been in Bethany Beach. She wondered if it had something to do with the warm, sea-breezy weather that she had also learned in earth science class develops due to differences in air pressure created by the differing heat capacities of water and dry land, a land where she wore far less clothing than she did at school, especially in the winter when students were bundled up in layers of flannel and wool.

Last summer, she had dated Kevin McGregor, a boy from her high school class whom she didn't know until she met him on the beach in Bethany on a day off from guard duty. Terri was trying to unfold her beach chair that would only open halfway.

"Need help?" asked a young man of average height with a pleasant, if unremarkable, face and sandy hair that was cut short and neat.

"Oh, this darn chair," Terri said with a shake of the head and a release of the chair as if to say, *All yours.*

He turned the low-to-the-ground chair upside down, studied the metal legs connection to the frame, and then gripped the metal rails on the seat. And with a quick flick of the wrists, the chair opened.

"Here you go." He squinted a look at Terri. "I think we were in the same graduation class at WJ."

"Really?"

"I had transferred in the middle of junior year. Other than playing on the tennis team, I was pretty much invisible."

"Walter Johnson is such a big school," Terri said with a little scrunch of her face.

"We were in Miss Topanian's eleventh-grade English class."

"Really?" Terri smiled. "I have to quit saying *really.*"

They exchanged names and summer job information. He was a waiter at a restaurant in Ocean View.

Kevin ended up sitting with Terri on the beach. He was majoring in business at the University of Vermont. "First semester, I got caught up in the parties and got probation. Then I settled down second semester. The party life has taken down many an unsuspecting freshman in Burlington."

They went out that night to Ocean City in Kevin's car. They walked the huge boardwalk, ate cotton candy, rode the bumper cars, and had an all-around good time. Kevin was not the outgoing sort, but not especially shy either, with a self-depreciating sense of humor. They were at the bottle toss, and on his last throw, he hit the two remaining wooden pins, which teetered but didn't fall.

"Such a burden to bear," he said with a lift of the brow to Terri, "to be in the supposed prime of my existence on this great, green earth and a physical failure all at once. Ah, the perplexities of life."

When Kevin took Terri home that evening, he walked her to the door and hesitated. She leaned forward and kissed him on the cheek.

"I had fun," she said.

"Me too," Kevin replied.

This was mid-July, and until toward the end of the summer season, they saw each other at least a couple times a week. They would go out for a casual meal—pizza, burgers, or occasionally a family restaurant—and afterward walk the boardwalk in Ocean City, Rehoboth Beach, or Bethany Beach, where they would talk.

Kevin had an intellectual depth that had snuck up on Terri. It was as though he had held it back, as if not wanting to show off. They talked about the unfairness of life, people who were born into money, and those who weren't.

"Rich kids take for granted what they have, while the poor scrap their way every waking hour," Kevin said one evening as they sat on the Bethany boardwalk with double-dipped chocolate chip ice cream cones in hand.

In late August, with their time nearing an end, Terri thought they were at a comfortable point in their relationship—passionate petting in his car—but Kevin never pushed it past second base, as it was implicitly understood that the fortress was off limits. Like herself, Terri assumed Kevin was also a virgin. Terri had thought it a nice time, but part of her was looking forward to returning to her life at school and her time with Kevin fading to a pleasant memory.

During Kevin's last week in Bethany, on the way back to Terri's house from a movie in Rehoboth Beach, Kevin asked, "How about for our last date of the summer we do dinner at Phillips and a round of miniature golf?"

"Only if we go Dutch, Kevin," Terri said. "Phillips Crab House is not cheap."

"It wouldn't seem right, Terri," Kevin said as he pulled the car in front of her house.

Terri looked at Kevin, sitting behind the wheel of his car. He had such a righteous glint in his eyes.

"Well, since this is the last time we will see each other for who knows when." She made a little squinty face. "Okay."

"What do you think," Kevin asked, "if I visited you during the school year? Our schools aren't that far apart."

"Oh," Terri said with little enthusiasm, which Kevin picked up on.

"Or," he said in a curt tone, "we can say it's been real and go on our merry way."

Their final evening together at Phillips followed by a round of miniature golf in Bethany Beach was a mostly silent affair. There had been limited conversation before the meal and silence during, with Kevin barely touching his crab cake platter.

On the third hole at miniature golf, Terri putted her ball between the rotating blades of the windmill and into the opening and out the other end, her ball trickling into the hole.

"How about that?" she asked, looking at Kevin for a reaction to her one-shot wonder.

"Nice shot," he said with little enthusiasm.

Over the course of the round, Terri made a couple more attempts at conversation but with little success. Kevin was going through the motions, speaking when spoken to, but with none of his wit or appreciation of Terri's company. He was wounded.

At the end of the evening, Kevin walked Terri to her front door. After a brief yet awkward silence, he said in a flat tone, "Good luck in school this year." He was facing Terri but not seeing her at all.

"Kevin," Terri said, looking at him.

He acknowledged Terri with a strained smile.

She reached for the door. "Same to you."

At the time, Terri had felt bad about the way it had ended last year, and she knew the onus was on her for how it had gone down. And Kevin had previously told her that next summer he would most likely only visit Bethany on the Fourth of July for sure and maybe Labor Day weekend since he would have to find a job back home.

"Need to make more and save for tuition." Kevin had taken out a college loan to help pay for school. He came from a large family of six kids, and they got by on his dad's salary as a government employee.

But last year she wasn't ready for a full-time commitment, and this year with Matt it seemed it was the other way around.

And did her last words to Matt—"To your *bang-bang* room?"—throw a wrench into their relationship? Matt's mouth had gaped open, and in his eyes was a look that said she wasn't playing fair, that this was all a summer game where certain rules of engagement were not to be crossed.

Where it had come from to speak like that to Matt was a little voice in her head, her Veronica voice telling her to give it to him straight. She needed to be careful what she blurted out before considering the consequences.

Unlike dating Kevin last year, Terri was a tad unsure of herself with Matt, whom she now considered untrustworthy. He was not whom she thought he was or, truth be told, had herself believe he was.

Kevin had been exactly whom she thought he was, someone who would have never asked her up to his *bang-bang* room. From time to time at school last year, Terri had thought about Kevin. But since arriving at the Bethany and especially since meeting Matt, she had thought little about him … until now. She did wonder whether he was coming up to Bethany for the big weekend. *Possibly.*

Kevin had been definitely more down to earth and true blue than Matt, who seemed to have shown his real colors last night, not only trying to get her upstairs but his answer to Brittany about the beach blast. When she had dated Kevin, she never worried about some other girl stealing him or Kevin pushing things on her in regard to sex.

But even so, Terri wasn't sure she was ready to give up on Matt. He was a guy after all, a jock, a stud lifeguard who was used to getting his way with girls. And maybe she shouldn't have brought up the *bang-bang* room. She knew at the time it would catch Matt off guard, but she had done it anyway. Terri sensed things were coming to a head, and this weekend would be where it would all play out.

A Hero emerges
From the throes of Hell
To vanquish the impudent
With no more than a Tell

The morning storm soon cleared. Terri rode her bike the short distance to the pool. She was looking forward to a chore in the pump room. Last summer, Terri had asked Greg to show her how to backwash the pool.

Greg had been surprised at her request. "I don't think Veronica has ever set foot in the pump room." He looked at her as if to say, *Really?*

A week later, before opening, Greg had found Terri in the pump room, turning off a pump and pulling the backwash valve.

"Sure you know what you're doing?" Greg asked over the whirling rumble of the motor and pumps impelling the rush of flowing water through the pipes.

"Simple enough procedure that you taught me," Terri said with a shrug. "A lever here, a lever there, reverse the water flow, and voila, the backwash complete. The filter clean. No unwanted contaminants."

"Ah," Greg said in a bewildered tone as though the idea of a girl doing or, even more so, wanting to do mechanical work was nearly incompressible. But he didn't stop her from backwashing. And this year, she had repaired a leaky skimmer with a putty knife and putty and re-caulked a gap between copingstones. In the girls' bathroom, she had carefully pulled three loose floor tiles with a chisel, scraped the existing mortar from the tiles and the floor, and cemented them back in place. Greg called her "the original handywoman."

Terri had an aptitude for anything mechanical. Her father had taught her the basics of working under the hood of a car, and she had changed a flat tire on a date once in high school when the boy hadn't a clue. She had considered majoring in engineering in college but took the easy way out and decided on history. Like most things in her life, school came easy to Terri.

When Terri arrived at the pump room, she found Greg inside. "Beat me to it, Greg."

Greg pulled a lever, triggering the rush of water reversing flow and then colliding with the roar of the pumps.

"I love the sound of a good backwash." He grinned and shrugged, as if to say, *Can't help myself.*

Entering his senior year at the University of Delaware, Greg was majoring in geology. He was a straight-arrow, crew cut–type guy who was an efficient manager yet with an offbeat sense of humor, telling corny jokes that one would expect from their parents' generation.

"Why did the geologist take his girlfriend to the quarry? He wanted to get a little boulder."

"I was going to tell a joke about fishing, but I forgot the line."

And he knew every knock-knock joke and even kept a notebook to record any joke he hadn't heard before. But off-color or dirty jokes, he recoiled from.

"Dirty words and sexual innuendos are the easy way out."

He was a bit of a by-the-books country boy without a trace of swagger. Greg was Terri's boss, but she also considered him a friend, even though they didn't socialize together. In a few years, she envisioned him settling down and getting married to a local girl, staying in Delaware, joining the American Legion, and volunteering for local charities. Every town needed people like Greg to keep the civic wheels turning.

Veronica was off today, and the other guard, Billy, had called in sick.

"Today shouldn't be too busy," Greg said as they exited the pump room, which was at the end of the clubhouse closest to the canal, "but we'll need all hands on deck this weekend."

But Greg's prediction was wrong. The pool was mobbed with kids, parents, grandparents, and younger couples with toddlers. It was as if every house in Bethany West had decided to go to the pool.

From eleven until three, Greg and Terri had to both man the guard chairs except on kids' swim break, which lasted fifteen minutes. So for one shift, Terri had to sit in the chair for nearly two hours. It was the busiest she had ever seen the pool. Every chair and umbrella table was in use.

Greg was constantly blowing his whistle. "Slow down ... No running ... No diving in the shallow end ... No balls in the water." Greg was like a little general in the chair, and Terri was glad of it.

Also there was a constant din of shouting voices coming from the pool in conjunction with groups of adults in loud, animated conversations. It appeared as if every child and adult were on an adrenaline rush. It was wild. Greg had to jump down from the chair and talk to two couples sitting at a table playing cards.

"Folks, please. You need to watch your language."

One of the men, a heavyset fellow in his mid-forties with a receding hairline and a thicket of dark hair on his chest that looked like a carpet, said, "Hey, kid, we're not bothering nobody." His words were slurred, and on the table were sixteen-ounce plastic cups packed with ice and a clear liquid, each with a slice of lime on the rim. It was early cocktail hour.

"Sir," Greg said in a voice that sounded much older than his years, "I am going to have to ask you to leave."

"My ass ain't going nowhere, sonny boy."

Greg offered the man a nod, as if to say, *Okay, if that's the way you want it.* He then walked over to Terri in the guard chair.

"Terri," Greg said in an even voice, "don't leave the chair unless to rescue someone. I have to make a call and will be right back."

While Greg was gone, the fat man's table got louder and more boisterous.

"You showed that punk kid, Tony," a woman with frizzy dyed red hair said.

"Big Tony," the fat man said, "don't take shit off nobody."

Now parents within earshot took notice. They were not happy. One mother came up to the guard chair and complained to Terri.

"Yes, ma'am," Terri said. "The manager is going to take care of it."

As the woman started to say something, both turned their attention to Greg and a policeman walking toward the fat man's table. The officer was tall and broad shouldered and looked like the second coming of John Wayne, dressed in a crisp blue short-sleeved uniform, spit-shined black boots, and a holstered gun on his hip. There was something in the way his eyes glinted that indicated he had dealt with much worse problems in his life.

The cop walked up to the table and silently motioned with his hand for Fat Tony to stand up. Tony remained sitting, eyeing the policeman.

"Mister," the policeman said in a deep, rumbly voice, "I'm going to give you one opportunity to obey me." He squinted a hard stare at Tony, his eyes now two slits. It was the look of a man who was very serious. "Or," he said in a scolding tone, "you will regret it for the rest of your life—however long that may be."

Beads of perspiration were emerging on Tony's forehead and upper lip. His arrogant disposition was gone, and in its place, the lips were pursed in a worried fret. The once-belligerent eyes looked around at his table of now silent compadres, all with an *oh-shit* look.

Tony stood.

The policeman said, "This way" and directed Tony toward the exit.

As they departed, a couple of tables applauded and offered their approval.

"Nice job, officer," one mother said with a toddler on her lap.

An elderly white-haired man sitting in a lounge chair spoke to the officer. "Military police, right?"

The cop looked over, his expression noncommittal.

"No?" the elderly man asked with a raised brow.

The policeman ignored the comment and led Tony through the clubhouse and to his awaiting squad car. And with that, everything was back to normal: the kids began hooting and shouting, the parents resumed their conversations, and Tony's tablemates packed up and silently departed.

By five thirty, only a few people remained. The pool was now empty. Terri and Greg were straightening up chairs, taking down umbrellas.

"Quite a day," Terri said to Greg.

"Yes." Greg snapped an umbrella latch, folding the canopy down. "Never had a day like this."

"That policeman was something else," Terri said.

"Jim Brewer," Greg said as they straightened the chairs of the corner table where Tony and his friends had sat. "Former Navy Seal. Two tours in Vietnam."

"Navy Seal?" Terri said as she began tossing in the trash can four plastic drink cups that were half-full, each with a slice of lemon sunken to the bottom. She took a whiff of the last one, noticing the gin and tonic.

"Yes, he's from my neighborhood just up the road in Ocean View." Greg slid a look over at Terri as if to gauge her interest.

She lifted her brow as if to say, *Please continue.*

"I was around ten when he returned from his second tour, but I still remember the look in his eyes as though he was there but not there. There was something almost ghostly about him." Greg lifted his chin toward a man who had entered the pool. "Let's keep an eye on him from here."

That was so unlike Greg, who was always by the book while on duty. Terri glanced at the man who was swimming laps in the top section of the T-shaped pool.

"You were saying," Terri said as they moved on to the last table.

"After a while, he came back, but not all the way." Greg reached up to bring the umbrella down, but the latch was stuck. "End of his first year back, he joined the Bethany Beach Police."

Greg strained to free the latch, and finally he removed the umbrella from the table hole and turned it upside down on the deck. He checked on the swimmer, who was exiting the pool via a ladder in the deep end.

"He's the real-deal cop." Greg gripped the umbrella pole with one hand, and with the other, he applied maximum force on the latch, which released. He put the folded umbrella back in the table hole. "Officer Brewer is Bethany's ace in the hole."

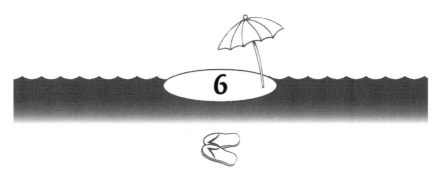

In the books written by the wise
There exists between the lines
The path for a life journey
That offers the sublime

During dinner at home with her mother—her father was coming in tomorrow for the holiday weekend—Terri received a call from Veronica about joining a group from the guard house to go to the Bottle and Cork in Dewey Beach, ten miles north of Bethany Beach.

Dewey Beach was the opposite of family-oriented Bethany Beach. During the summer, it was overrun by a crowd in their early twenties. Every summer the locals were up in arms about the noise and at times rowdiness, but then the season ended, and all was quiet until the following summer rolled around.

"Veronica, I am staying in to catch up on my summer reading for school."

Veronica, who attended a state school in western Maryland, reminded Terri that she didn't have any required reading.

"Have fun, and don't forget your phony ID," Terri said through a laugh.

The last time they went, Veronica forgot hers and ended up sneaking in through the window to the girls' bathroom.

After hanging up the phone, Terri wondered if Matt were going and, if so, why he hadn't asked her himself. Possibly he was upset about the *bang-bang* room comment she had made to him, or perhaps it was because she hadn't allowed their relationship to advance to a more personal level.

An image of Matt and Veronica drawn together by some irresistible magnetic force, two beautiful creatures speaking a silent language of undeniable attraction, rose for an instant in Terri's mind before her mother said, "Terri, come and finish your dinner before it gets cold."

After dinner, Terri went out to the screened-in porch on the side of the house. Her yard and most of the other yards in Bethany West were similar small patches of grass between utilitarian, ordinary-looking houses, summer cottages really. Only a smattering of homes were year-round. There was a scattering of sapling trees here and there in her view. She had learned from Greg that Bethany West had previously been a farm, which explained the dearth of big trees.

"A cornfield ran along what is now Collins Avenue," Greg had told Terri earlier in the year as they departed the pool at closing. "My friends and I used to run barefoot through the rows of tall stalks, playing hide-and-go-seek.

At the bike rack, Greg had looked around as though seeing his youth. "What fun it all was back then."

Terri pulled her bike from its station but stopped as she sensed Greg had more to say.

"But," he said through a remembering sigh, "times change. As do people."

Terri wondered if Bethany West, over time, wouldn't change: additions added to homes, little touches such as ivy-covered arbors and pergolas leading to stone or brick patios, or outdoor planters and flower pots here and there to give the yards a homier feel. Terri's backyard did have an appealing octagon-shaped purple martin birdhouse atop a pole that reminded her of a mini-mansion. There was a porch surrounding each of the four levels, an overhanging roof, and a white railing running along each gallery that the little birds—varying in color from iridescent dark purple to a lighter purple to a brownish color—used as a perch before entering the small entry holes with insects in their beaks to feed their young.

There were few fences in Bethany West, and it provided a certain sense of freedom, as though the neighborhood was one big family until the end of the season when, like the purple martins, they migrated away until returning next year.

The hurried shouts of a boy could be heard from the house that backed up to Terri's. The house was on Poplar Court, the street that the swimming pool was on. The screen door burst open, and a boy followed by his father came out into the backyard with a baseball and gloves.

Terri recognized them from the pool. The boy, no more than ten, was Timmy, whose mother had made him come out of the pool to wait a full thirty minutes after lunch before swimming. *Mo-o-om.*

Father and son silently caught and tossed the ball back to the other. There was something timeless, so traditionally American about this simple exercise. Someday she might have a son like Timmy, a daughter, or both. Someday Terri and family might well own a home here in Bethany West and come full circle when she would tell her son or daughter to do something displeasing to them. And then she would be on the receiving side. *Mo-o-om.*

Terri turned her attention to her reading assignment. She opened *The Grapes of Wrath* by John Steinbeck, which she was over halfway through. The hardships people dealt with during the Great Depression were diametrically opposed to the carefree life Terri and her friends lived.

Terri's parents had lived through the Depression as children. Her mother, Betty, nee Elizabeth O'Brien, was one of three daughters to a police sergeant in Chicago. She didn't feel the brunt of it like her husband, who was one of four boys living in the heartland.

Richard Landers was born in the farmhouse of his family's wheat farm in Lawrence, Kansas. When Richard was five, the family lost the 160-acre farm, packed up essentials in the back of the family truck, and, with five dollars to their name, moved to Wichita, staying with relatives until Richard's father, who was gifted mechanically, got a job working in a plant building airplanes. Richard Landers had told Terri on more than one occasion that she had received her mechanical aptitude from her grandfather.

But things got real tough when Richard's father died of a heart attack when Richard was ten. His mother took on work ironing and sewing. All the boys worked. Richard, who was the youngest, delivered newspapers in the morning and worked weekends delivering flowers on his bicycle all over town.

When World War II arrived, Richard joined the navy at age seventeen. After four years of service, mostly as an antiaircraft gunner on a destroyer in the Pacific, he went to college on the GI Bill and made a life for himself.

Terri learned her father's history from her mother. Her father never once initiated with his daughter a conversation about his youth or the war. Terri once overheard her father say to her mother over their evening cocktail that growing up during the Depression made him appreciate what he had today.

Richard Landers worked for the Department of Commerce as an accountant. When Terri once asked if he enjoyed his job, Richard had replied, "It's safe and secure work with a reliable pension down the road. That's all that matters."

Terri remembered the matter-of-fact tone of her father's voice. It was the voice of a man who had seen hard times and was wary of risk. She wondered if only having one child, Terri, were another way of avoiding risk.

But the Okie migrants in Steinbeck's book existed at another level of difficult times compared to any other group of people during the Great Depression: folks escaping the Dust Bowl in great numbers toward California, living outdoors, bathing in rivers, and having little or no money as well as no security or backup plan. It was California or bust.

It was difficult to fully appreciate and understand what people less fortunate had gone through. And even today, like Officer Jim Brewer, who had evicted Fat Tony from the pool, Terri wondered what sort of demons he had rattling around in his head from two tours in Vietnam.

Finish the book, Terri said to herself as she opened to a new chapter that began, "The moving, questing people were migrants now."

**Whom amongst us who has lived
Has not been delivered a blow
By someone near and dear
Fermenting revaluation of all we know**

The intermittent beeps of the alarm clock woke Terri at seven. She turned it off and lay back in bed, tempted to slide back down into a warm sleep, not having finished the Steinbeck book until one thirty in the morning. But she fought the temptation, sat up on the side of her bed, and stretched her arms overhead with her fingers interlaced.

A slant of sunshine peeped through the blinds, and with it the sleepiness faded. She had dreamt that she and a blurry image of her grandmother Landers were with the Joad family rattling out of the Dust Bowl, packed like sardines in a rickety old truck.

Her grandmother, who died when Terri was eleven and whom she had only met twice, kept saying in the dream, "Ain't one damn thing fair in this life, Granddaughter. Remember that."

Terri had set the alarm early to swim laps at the pool before opening. And with *The Grapes of Wrath* still hanging over her literally like a bad dream, she decided that swimming would clear her head.

She took off her lightweight flannel nightgown and changed into her traditional dark blue one-piece women's lifeguard suit. She slipped into a matching Bethany West guard T-shirt with *Lifeguard* scrolled below *Bethany West* on the left chest pocket over her suit.

The Grapes of Wrath was on her dresser; next to it were her two other assigned books: a biography of Edgar Allan Poe, which she had already read, and one on Abraham Lincoln.

Terri had previously read a biography on Lincoln in high school, but never before Poe, whose poem "The Raven" she had read in twelfth-grade English class and found hauntingly beautiful. Poe's life, much like his writing, was brilliantly strange and troubling. He was found wandering the streets of Baltimore delirious, wearing another man's clothes, and he died mysteriously four days later of unknown causes at the age of forty.

Poe could have written his mysterious death into a fascinating novel or even a poem. How different Poe's life might have been if he hadn't lost his parents at a young age. He might have had a happy life, but possibly at the risk of his brilliant writing career. Did his pain contribute to his writing? Or could he have been a brilliant writer and happy too?

Guess it will remain unknown, Terri thought as she took a quick look at herself in the mirror before beginning her day.

Terri stood at the deep end of the T-section of the pool. She tucked her hair into her swim cap. She would have preferred not to wear it, but Greg would get upset if he saw her without it on since caps were required to be worn by women in the pool.

She liked to start freestyle, then go into breaststroke, and end it with the backstroke, but no butterfly, which she always hated. She went through forty-five minutes of stroke after stroke, only interrupted by turns.

After finishing her laps, Terri swam out of the T-section, headed down to the shallow end, and exited, where she was greeted by Veronica, who was collecting debris from the pool surface with a leaf skimmer.

"You missed a great time last night," Veronica said as Terri dried herself off.

"Give me a minute." Terri tossed the towel and swim cap on a nearby chair and slipped back into her T-shirt.

She then went to the storage closet in the front of the clubhouse and retrieved the pool vacuum. At the edge of the pool, she attached the vacuum hose to the vacuum head and submerged it in the pool.

"There were five of us, one couple and two other guards. Kirk drove us in his big old Woodie." Veronica slanted a look at Terri. "Matt decided to come at the last minute." There was a hint of conspiratorial intrigue in her voice.

Terri said with her eyes, *Go on.* She had a shuddering vision of Veronica and Matt sitting in the back seat of Kirk's station wagon, shoulder to shoulder, laughing and chatting, and each suddenly absorbed in his or her charisma and beauty. And she remembered Veronica's words. "I can only imagine how hard Matt is to resist."

Veronica went on to say that there was a band playing on the patio of the Bottle and Cork. "We all danced and drank shooters. Had us a grand old time."

A knot pulled tight in Terri's stomach as she sensed there was more to this story, but she only nodded as she pulled the vacuum hose for more slack, moving the vacuum head along the shallow end.

"Did you know that Matt's a great dancer?" Veronica said. "And *sooo* funny." She dumped debris from the leaf skimmer into a rubber trash can.

Terri stopped vacuuming and turned back to look at Veronica. *Was my thought the other day of Veronica stealing a boy from an unsuspecting girl, without a hitch, now coming to fruition?* Now Terri wondered if she were the unsuspecting or, more precisely, the suspecting girl.

"Yes," Terri said, "he's a funny kinda guy when the mood strikes him."

"Yeah ..." Veronica began to yawn. Covering her mouth with the back of her wrist, she went on through the yawn, "He most certainly is."

By mid-afternoon, the pool was teeming with kids of all ages, parents, grandparents, and a few young couples without children. It was a noisy group but well behaved, other than a few boys pushing the envelope in regard to horseplay in the pool and running on deck.

Billy, the fourth guard, was in the guard chair and blowing his whistle and shouting for kids to slow down. He had two boys sitting under the guard chair for a fifteen-minute time-out for disregarding his second warning for splashing each other and other people in the pool.

He had come a long ways from his first week guarding the pool. Billy attended the local high school and, at first, was shy, not only with the other guards but about blowing his whistle when needed. He was not assertive in the chair. The kids sensed this and began to ignore him.

Greg had spoken with him about it. "Politely but forcefully. When you sit in that chair, you must let them know who is in charge."

Everything changed for Billy during his second week when two boys were splashing each other in the shallow end and Billy meekly blew his whistle for them to stop. The boys paused for a moment, looked at Billy, laughed in his face, and proceeded to continue to splash.

Terri and Greg were checking over a faulty skimmer in the baby pool. Terri asked if they should intervene, and Greg told her, "He has to learn to handle this on his own."

And so he did. Billy glanced over at Terri and Greg and then the boys, and it was as if a light bulb turned on in his eyes. Billy blew his whistle with gusto. *preeeeeeet*

He said in a strong voice, a tone Terri had never heard from him before, "Get out of the pool now. Both of you." He extended his arm at the boys, finger-wriggling for them to come.

His sixteen-year-old freckled face was now that of someone older, a person in charge. The boys got right out of the pool and sat down under the guard chair, without a peep from either.

Terri thought it funny how Billy could change so suddenly from a shy, meek boy to one in control. She also wondered what had gotten into Veronica. She had always been a bit aloof and impersonal, but Terri had always thought of her as a fair and decent person. But the way she had hinted this morning at something going on with Matt was unnerving.

Maybe I am overreacting. Maybe. But the thought of Veronica and Matt together and what a beautiful couple they would make, Aphrodite and Adonis, sparked something. Had a combination of animal magnetism, alcohol, and the outdoor scene under the influence of a rock band triggered something between Veronica and Matt?

Looking back on her friendship with Veronica, they were an odd pairing. Competitive swimming had brought them together, and though Veronica was a strong swimmer, she was never at the level of Terri.

Terri's arrival on the swim team at Kenwood had knocked Veronica's status down a couple pegs. For all those years, had Veronica been seething about losing meet after meet to Terri? And did Veronica finally decide to beat Terri in a competition that she was the more talented? It was hard to know because a part of Veronica was an enigma.

But it was their differences that Terri always thought made the friendship unique. Opposites attract. But were Veronica's hints about her and Matt her way of letting Terri down easy? Had she stolen her summer beau, or was Terri letting her imagination get the best of her?

Terri was fond of Matt and did enjoy being in the company of a studly guy, but she was never close to being in love. Though there was a certain status to dating Matt, a position that she had to admit she enjoyed a lot. She noticed the glances of admiration from other girls on the beach while he sat perched up in the guard chair or when they walked down the boardwalk holding hands as other girls stole envious peeks at Matt.

Even so, Terri had never been head over heels with Matt, though part of her dilemma was that, if Matt had wanted to get serious, such as wanting to see her over the school year, would she have gone for it or declined? But that may well be a moot point since it was becoming uncomfortably clear that Matt was out for a good time and nothing more. The most comfortable she had ever been was last summer with Kevin, her boy from Bethesda.

It was a busy day at the pool as Terri, Veronica, and Billy worked two guard chairs for most of the afternoon while Greg repaired a leaky pump in the pump room. In a way, it was a blessing since Terri didn't have time to dwell on Veronica and Matt.

But by late that Friday afternoon, the skies had clouded up. They weren't rain clouds, but enough to encourage folks at the pool to call it a day. Billy had departed an hour ago, so it was now only Terri and Veronica at the pool. Greg was in the guard room, tending to next week's schedule and ordering supplies.

Veronica was in the guard chair. One family remained, but they were packing up to leave. Terri began pushing chairs into tables and taking down the umbrellas, while Veronica remained in the guard chair, watching an empty pool.

Veronica brought to Terri's mind a line from "The Raven" by Poe. "Perched, and sat, and nothing more." Much like Poe's mysterious poem, there was an aura of dark splendor about Veronica, something unknowing, even to herself that might eventually reveal itself. Or maybe it already had.

Terri moved from table to table, ignoring Veronica, still in the guard chair. If she had more to say, Terri would listen, but she had no inclination to initiate conversation. Terri moved around a table, tucking in the aluminum frame chairs.

"How did the summer reading go?"

Terri hadn't noticed Veronica approach. Veronica reached up and loosened the umbrella hinge, dropping the canopy. She looked at Terri with

43

a look Terri had come to know: attentiveness with a trace of indifferent concern. *So Veronica.*

"I finished *The Grapes of Wrath.*" Terri squinted a look at Veronica, trying to ascertain if anything had gone on with Matt last night. She considered asking her, but her instincts told her to let it play out.

"Good," Veronica said in a tone, indicating next order of business. "Forgot to tell you, I saw your old flame from last summer, Kevin, at the Cork last night. He and a friend are camping out at Indian River Inlet for the weekend."

"Really."

"He asked about you."

Terri silently moved on to the next table.

"Matt overheard and asked who he was." Veronica was trying to unsnap the umbrella hinge but couldn't get it to release.

Terri reached up from the other side of the table, slipped her finger under Veronica's, and snapped the hinge loose, allowing the canopy to fall. "And?"

Veronica offered an indifferent shrug. "I told him you two dated for a while last summer before you broke it off."

Terri breathed deeply. Worlds were colliding.

**Under the cover of darkness
The children do play
With the emotions of others
Whom they intend to slay**

After work, Terri decided to ride her bike around Bethany West to let things sink in. Instead of turning right for home, she turned left on Half Moon Circle and began a slow, steady ride around the neighborhood: down Collins Avenue, weaving around Fenwood Circle that ran inside of Half Moon Circle, heading back up Collins Avenue briefly, and then down Radial Circle that ran inside of Fenwood Circle, semicircles within semicircles.

Veronica had also told Terri that Matt had invited Kevin to the second keg party of the week at the guard house this evening. "Matt called it a full-bore Friday bash," Veronica had said with a straight face, nary an inkling of offense at the designation. She had gone on to say that she wondered if Matt even remembered. "He was pretty wasted by that point."

Part of Terri didn't want to go to the party, the fragment that didn't need the drama of Matt and Kevin in the same room with her and of course Veronica, who was "so looking forward to tonight." The way she had said it was like an actress over-emoting.

But the other part, the stronger portion of Terri, encouraged herself to attend. First, unlike Veronica, she could read Matt and determine if anything had gone on between them. She wished she didn't have to pursue this, but it gnawed on her. Her mother told her once when she was a little girl, "Loyalty is about as important a quality a person can have in a friendship."

Betty had been tucking in her seven-year-old daughter after reading

The Wolves of Willoughby Chase, a children's book about two girl cousins who escape a prison-like orphanage and had only each other to depend on.

But an even more surprising reason was that Terri wanted to see Kevin. It was not to make Matt jealous, but she missed his even-keel, steady-as-you-go demeanor. He was a drama-free, trustworthy guy. He was nothing flashy, just a good guy with a keen and inquisitive mind. It was the conversations that she missed most.

Kevin saw big-picture scenarios in life. He never spoke too specifically, but more a general intellectual understanding and comprehension of the human condition. "People talk about the fifties as being a great time to live. Yeah, if you were white."

In her bedroom, Terri changed into a turquoise T-shirt with *Bethany Beach* scrolled in dark blue across the front, khaki shorts, and flip-flops, her basic summer attire. She was meeting Veronica at her house at quarter to seven, and from there, they would ride their bikes into town before the party. Here they were young adults, and still they rode their bicycles. And Terri liked the fact that a part of her childhood was still with her.

I will always ride my bike in Bethany, she thought as she looked at herself in her bedroom mirror.

She placed her fingertips on her prominent cheekbones, bringing her fingers down and touching at her chin, which her grandmother Landers had told her was "a Landers chin, strong and determined." Her golden tan accentuated her eyes, which Kevin once described as "blue like the ocean after a storm." Her dark brown hair was parted down the middle and fell almost to her shoulders. A smile skipped across her face. She liked the way she looked, pretty in a wholesome way.

Terri now accepted that she would never be described as glamorous or that she had the look or body type that drew men's eyes like Veronica, which Terri was glad of. She didn't want or need that type of attention.

Terri heard the crunch of car tires on gravel and peeked out the window. Her father's car was pulling into the driveway. She watched him as he got out of the car, went to the trunk, and removed his suitcase. Richard Landers was still wearing a white short-sleeved shirt and tie, which was loosened. He had departed early from work and driven directly to the beach.

There was a weariness that seemed to always drape over her father, a no-nonsense sort of man who at the age of fifty-two had the look of someone going through the motions. He had thirteen more years to work before retiring.

"A lifetime," Terri overheard him comment recently to her mother during their daily cocktail before dinner. Terri wondered if the Great Depression and then the war, which he never ever spoke of, had sapped some of the spirit from her father's being. She rarely heard her father laugh, though his mood and demeanor would pick up after the Washington Redskins won a big game. Football or, more correctly, the Redskins were her father's one big passion. Everything else seemed like duty or obligation.

But financially, they must be better off than other families with a boatload of children. Terri had received a partial academic scholarship to college, and her parents lived a frugal life, other than Kenwood Country Club and coming to Bethany Beach every summer.

She hoped her parents would buy their beach rental. She felt they would, and after her father retired, they would spend a good deal of time here, especially in summer and autumn, and enjoy the slower-paced life in Bethany Beach, where her father did let his hair down a bit, drinking more than one cocktail before dinner, socializing at the local VFW in Ocean View, and coming home in a cheery mood.

Earlier this summer, Terri had attended a let-the-season-begin barbeque at the home of a man Richard had met last summer at bingo at the VFW. Irv Hudson was similar in age to her father, a salt-of-the-earth type of man who had lived his entire life in Ocean View other than serving in the war. Like her father, Irv was a quiet man, but with an observant quick wit.

On the way home from the barbeque, Richard commented on Irv. "No frills. No BS. Just a solid, dependable man. My kind of guy."

It was not only Irv but his VFW friends who had attended the party that Terri sensed might attract her father to retire here, a group of taciturn, resilient men.

"We could use men of that quality working for our government," Richard said as turned off Half Moon Circle onto their street. Terri could not remember her father being so effusive.

Bethany Beach and its people are good medicine for my dad, Terri thought as she went to the front door and greeted her father with a hug.

"Hi, Daddy," she said through a welcoming smile.

Richard forced a smile. The fatigue from work and driving in Friday afternoon traffic still lurked over him. "Hello, honey."

Terri's mother was in the kitchen preparing dinner. She turned and looked through the kitchen hatch, an opening that was below the cabinets and above the countertop, over the three-stool bar that divided the two spaces.

She smiled at her husband. "Cocktail, dear?"

Richard lifted his brow to his daughter, his lips splitting into a thin, knowing grin. "Thought you'd never ask, Betty."

Richard made his way through the dining space into the kitchen, where his wife welcomed him with a kiss on the lips and handed him a martini, garnished with an olive.

"Ah," he said with a lift in his voice, "a working man's best friend." He took a seat in the living room at the front of the house.

The house had three bedrooms and two baths, all situated off the hallway. And that was basically it, along with the porch, living room–dining room, kitchen, and an outdoor shower in the back.

"Mom," Terri said, "okay to skip dinner tonight?"

Betty leaned forward with her hands on the countertop. "Terri, don't you want to spend time with your father?"

"Betty," Richard said from his easy chair, "let the girl go and live her life."

Terri shot a look at her mother, who had come into the living room with martini in hand.

She smiled back at Terri. "What's on schedule for this evening?"

Terri didn't want to lie but didn't want to mention the party at the guard house, not that her parents wouldn't allow it, but her mother might worry. "Going into town with Veronica for subs. Maybe run into some kids from WJ."

Betty nodded an okay at Terri and then turned her attention to her husband. "Richard, let's sit on the porch. Those adorable baby martins are spreading their wings."

He who had been invisible
Comes knocking at my door.
Upon answering
I realize he is not
Nevermore.

Terri's rental house had four bicycles that were kept at a bike rack in the backyard. Both girls' bikes were too small, so Terri rode a three-speed yellow Schwinn boy's bike with a basket in front.

Since there were no hills in Bethany Beach, she kept it in second gear everywhere she rode, including now on her way over to Veronica's house. Like many of the homes in Bethany West, Terri's was on a cul-de-sac, as was Veronica's, two blocks from Terri's and on the way to town.

Terri rode up to the front of Veronica's home. Terri was about to dismount her bike when a shadow said from inside the screened-in front porch, "Be right there."

The screen door opened. *Oh boy.* Veronica appeared wearing a pair of tight jean shorts and a bright yellow halter top with a dip along the front, exposing a tantalizing crevice of her bulging cleavage. *Where did this outfit come from?*

As Veronica approached, walking her bike, Terri saw that she was wearing eyeliner and mascara, her eyes aglow like emeralds. She looked stunningly, vampishly beautiful, her raven-black hair lush and wavy.

The one time Terri and Veronica had previously worn makeup was at the WJ senior prom. And the morning after, Veronica had called Terri. "We were painted ladies last night."

"I felt self-conscious all night," Terri said, "as though I were wearing a mask."

"I looked at myself in the mirror this morning," Veronica replied through a sigh.

Terri envisioned the overdramatic expression on Veronica's face. "Me too."

"Men don't wear makeup, so why should we?" Veronica said in a matter-of-fact tone. "So let's make a pact never to wear that hideous war paint again. Leave it to the socs."

Normally Terri would have mentioned Veronica's makeup and asked about her outfit, but not now. Not since she wasn't sure about her and Matt and whatever was going on with Veronica. No, it was better to let it play out and allow Veronica's free will take her where it may.

At the edge of her gravel driveway, Veronica came to a halt. "I hear some of the WJ soc girls are staying in Ocean City this weekend." Veronica's eyes were on Terri, seeking a response.

"Haven't seen any of them since Christmas break. I hope we see them." Terri's dying tone belied her words.

"You're interested in seeing the *social* girls?" Veronica spoke the word *social* with a special twist as though she was putting a spin on a ball.

"We were friends with them in high school. Sorta." Terri shrugged.

Veronica slid her leg through the open frame of her sleek purple bike, straddling her legs on both sides for a moment before mounting. "I thought we agreed last Christmas to move on from all their pretentious nonsense," she said as they began pedaling up the street.

Veronica could have been queen of the soc girls in high school, a group of seven or so, many of whom by twelfth grade were dating guys in college. They ate lunch at the same table in the cafeteria every day, and between classes they would cluster for brief private chats in front of a hallway locker before scurrying off to their next class.

Veronica and Terri had been invited to eat lunch with them at the start of senior year. Veronica fit right in, putting on a calm, cool, sometimes-interested or sometimes-not performance that was worthy of an award. Terri, on the other hand, spoke when spoken to and initiated little conversation. She was a bit unsettled in their company—part of her wanting to be accepted and another wanting no part of this girl clique.

Next day, Veronica told Terri that she didn't want to join the socs for lunch anymore, and Terri went along. They did see them at parties and football and basketball games, where some of the socs performed as cheerleaders. So by the end of high school, Terri and Veronica were on friendly terms with the socs but by no way were they friends, just acquaintances.

Though if Veronica had been willing, Terri would have ventured into the social swirl of the socs, but at the time, she didn't have the confidence to go it alone. And part of her wondered if it weren't being the best friend of the gorgeous, confident Veronica that made her acceptable.

Terri had been uncertain in the midst of this cliquish girl-talk scene, which had an exclusive vibe that reeked of, *We are superior.* On one hand, she thought it ridiculous, but another conflicted part of her still wanted acceptance.

Veronica, who couldn't have cared less about acceptance, would chitchat with the in-crowd from time to time, but at the same time, she kept a distance, an impenetrable wall of never knowing for certain what exactly she was really thinking.

At a bike rack in town, they locked their bikes and walked a half block up toward the ocean to the submarine shop. On the way, Veronica received three full head turns of admiration from men, one pushing a toddler in a stroller with his wife, who jerked his arm and scolded, "Hank!"

The Yellow Submarine, a two-story no-frills sandwich joint with mellow-yellow storefront siding, was a popular hangout for junior high and high school students. After ordering cheesesteaks, fries, and large Cokes in sixteen-ounce Styrofoam cups packed with ice, the girls took their trays upstairs to a seating area, a quieter option from the din below crowded with families of young noisy children and packs of teenyboppers.

They sat in a booth with a view of the street below. People, families mostly, were bustling about, along with the ubiquitous teenyboppers, who were racing to and fro with the anticipatory excitement of what the evening might hold, possibly a spontaneous gathering on the beach, meeting an interesting someone, or just the freedom of running loose and free in Bethany Beach.

On occasion, the subs could be stringy and way too greasy, but tonight their cheesesteaks and fries were piping hot, moist, and delicious. Halfway through the silent meal—with Veronica seemingly unaware of anything out of kilter in their relationship or at least acting that way—two guys came up the steps with trays of food. To Terri's surprise, it was Kevin with another boy, whom she didn't recognize.

Kevin spotted Terri and smiled his easy grin. "Well," Kevin said with a lift in his voice as he came up to the table. His eyes were fixed on Terri, aware of Veronica but not acknowledging her presence.

In a split-second pause, Terri intuited that something awkward had transpired between Kevin and Veronica. *The Bottle and Cork and Matt the other night?*

"Hi, Kevin," Terri said. "Good to see you."

Terri lifted her gaze to Kevin's friend, who stood next to him, though back a half step. He was tall and slender with a thicket of dark curly hair. He had an expectant and inquiring slant to his eyebrows, as if waiting for the next move.

"This is Josh," Kevin said with a tilt of his head.

"Hello, Josh. Terri," she replied as she placed her fingertips against her chest. "And my friend Veronica."

Josh nodded a hello to Terri and then turned his attention to Veronica, who was casually sipping her Coke through a straw. She lifted her brow, offering him a look, the beautiful, temperamental princess appraising.

"We met the other night at the Bottle and Cork," Josh said to Veronica. There was something unhurried and privileged in his voice, possibly East Coast prep school.

Veronica made a face. *We did?*

"Would you like to join us?" Terri offered her hand for Kevin to sit next to her.

Kevin placed his tray on the table and slid in next to Terri. "Let me guess," he continued with a knowing smile. "After this, you're going to the party at the guard house."

"That's the plan." Terri looked up at Josh, still standing as though uncertain if he should sit or not.

Finally Josh said to Veronica. "May I?"

"Be my guest," Veronica answered as she slid over.

Kevin mentioned that Josh was his roommate at Vermont. "He looks like a bookworm, but there is a party animal lurking below the surface,"

Kevin said with a smiling glance at Josh before sinking his teeth into his cold cut sub.

Kevin and Terri caught up on the past year. Kevin had decided to major in political science. "It has more of a human interest appeal than business, which seems so cold."

Josh was also a poly sci major. "I would like to get my law degree and then get a job working on Capitol Hill. Hoping to get an internship there next year."

Veronica looked at Josh, as though seeing him for the first time. "I bet you want to run for office at some point."

Josh furrowed his brow. The eyes registered an inquiring attentiveness. "Possibly."

"He already sounds like a politician, doesn't he?" Kevin asked to the table.

"Politics is a noble cause," Veronica said with an air of conviction, "if one has the best interest of one's constituents."

"Yes," Kevin added, "but sometimes the temptation of money, power, or *sex* can ruin the best of intentions." He said the word *sex* with a twist of emphasis as though to make a point.

"So I've heard," Veronica said to Kevin through a Cheshire cat smile before taking a ravenous bite of her steak and cheese.

10

**It is there before me,
The stabling of my back,
But I choose to ignore it
As I recalibrate my tack**

After finishing their subs, they decided to take a stroll up the north end of the boardwalk before heading over to the guard party. Terri and Kevin were in front; Veronica and Josh were a few paces behind.

After a couple of blocks, Terri and Kevin turned to check on their friends.

"Where did they go?" Terri looked back through a steady stream of people coming up and down the boardwalk. They moved over to the railing.

Kevin glanced down the boardwalk and then looked out at the ocean as waves crested one after another, crashing onto the beach. "I've thought a lot about how we departed last year." He turned his attention to Terri. "It was just that you were the first girl I …" He sighed. "I wish I hadn't come on so strong." He stared at his hands and then back at the water.

"I shouldn't have been so brusque with you." Terri placed her fingertips on the edge of the top rail. Far out on the horizon, the dark outline of a tanker seemed frozen in place between water and sky. "I enjoyed our time together last year." She looked up to see Josh and Veronica approaching, each with an ice cream cone and a look of comfort in each other's company.

As they neared, Terri noticed that Veronica was no longer wearing makeup. Terri wondered how she pulled that off. *Public restroom off the boardwalk?*

Terri flashed a questioning glance at Veronica, who responded with a squinty look and a tweak of her nose that suggested *my mistake* before her expression forwarded itself back to self-assured Veronica.

"When Josh runs for office," Veronica said as she and Josh came to a halt alongside Terri and Kevin, "I told him I would volunteer for his campaign." She took a hearty lick of her double-scoop chocolate ice cream and then another.

She smiled at Terri. *Isn't this great?*

All four were silent for a moment as though recalibrating their relationships and status. "We've decided," Josh said with a nod, "that we are going to pass on the party at the guard house."

"Fine by me." Kevin looked at Terri.

Terri was also fine with it. She wanted to be with Kevin and wanted to put Matt and whatever happened with Veronica stored away to be revisited at a later date.

"Let's go to the Ocean City boardwalk." She looked around for confirmation.

"I'm in," Kevin replied.

Josh and Veronica exchanged looks.

Josh said, "Us too."

They drove the twenty-five-minute drive south in Kevin's two-door Chevy Corvair coupe, the same car he had last summer. Kevin had bought it used his senior year of high school from a neighbor with money he had saved mowing lawns.

"GM stopped making the Corvair a while back," Kevin had told Terri on their first date last year, heading to the same destination as they were this evening. "A few years after the Mustang came out, it was decided the Corvair wasn't sleek enough." He tapped his hand affectionately on the dashboard. "I think there are character lines all the way around the entire car. They're just more subtle." He looked at Terri as though to gauge her interest.

She made a face indicating, *Please continue.*

"Someday, in my opinion," Kevin had said with a lift of his chin, "this car will be a classic, though probably overlooked by many."

Kevin's car was smaller and more compact than Matt's behemoth, but Terri now felt an immediate level of comfort sitting in the bucket seat, inhaling its distinct old car smell of vinyl upholstery and carpet. Matt's car wasn't as old, but Terri had no recollection of its details other than how big it was, dangerously big.

Josh and Veronica were in the back seat, holding hands. Josh offered a political bon mot from time to time. "If con is the opposite of pro, then isn't Congress the opposite of progress?"

Veronica laughed. "Oh, that is so true, Josh." She leaned up front between Kevin and Terri. "Smart and witty guy," she said as she sat back and tilted her head against Josh's for a moment.

Kevin shot a look at Terri. *What is going on with Veronica?* Terri looked over her shoulder. It was a reflex motion, almost to make sure it was really Veronica back there. Veronica offered a big smile to Terri, a radiant beam of infatuation.

The boardwalk in Ocean City was teeming with people, who were of a different ilk from Bethany Beach folks. It was a rougher-looking blue-collar crowd, men in tank tops and some with tattoos on their arms. There were women wearing their hair in beehives as though they were still back in the sixties. There was a smattering of more upscale people, like those in Bethany Beach with little kids in tow. There were also college kids, but other young adults were loud and boisterous, and the guys had a swagger about them as though they were looking for a fight. Terri hadn't noticed this before, or it was not as pronounced as it seemed tonight.

"The rednecks come out of the woodwork the week of the Fourth," Kevin said in a low voice to Terri.

But what she had always noticed—and especially tonight—was the boardwalk smells that were similar to Bethany, but everything about this two-mile stretch of wooden planks was bigger and stronger: the aroma of funnel cakes, popcorn, and french fries mingling with the breezy salt air. And the wider beach and ocean seemed darker and somehow more ominous than the view from Bethany.

They stopped at Spill the Milk booth.

"Ah," Kevin said, "the scene of my past humiliation."

The four of them stood behind a young couple. The guy in long pants and a tank top exposed a beet-red sunburn on his shoulders. His hair was cut military short, and like a badge of honor, he sported a USMC tattoo in dark blue ink on his left bicep. He was of medium size with a lean and muscular build.

The girl had a sharp chin, a thin and pointed nose, and curly dark hair that she wore short like an undisciplined pageboy. She had on cutoffs and a white T-shirt with *Semper Fidelis* scrolled across the front and the Marine Corps emblem of an eagle, globe, and anchor below the inscription. She reminded Terri of a sassy waitress at a diner.

The young marine took the first ball and reared back and fired a bullet at the wooden bottles, stacked one atop the other two, knocking down the top bottle. He threw again and missed, causing him to shake his head and mumble something inaudible under his breath. His final toss hit in the middle of the two bottles, rattling them, but they remained standing.

"What?" the marine hollered. "I hit them dead center."

The man behind the booth was a heavyset, seen-it-all sort of guy with thinning dark hair and a three-day growth of beard. "Another try?"

"Come on, darlin'," the girl said, grabbing her guy's hand. "Let's not waste any more money on this rip-off."

The man behind the booth turned his attention to Terri's group. "Whatdaya say, fellas. Win a prize for one of the pretty ladies." He offered a quick smile to Terri and then to Veronica, to whom he did a double take as though he had seen something rare. It was not a lustful look but more that of a connoisseur of beautiful women.

"Go on, Kevin," Terri said. "Give it another shot."

"Sounds like a plan," Kevin answered as he paid the man.

Terri noticed the bottom bottles were offset just a bit and figured that was part of the difficulty in bringing all of them down.

Terri whispered in Kevin's ear, "Hit between the top pin and one of the bottom ones."

Kevin's first throw hit right where Terri suggested and knocked down two bottles. He looked at her and said loud enough for the man to hear, "I am going to aim at the top of the bottle. The bottom is where the suckers live."

Kevin made a smiley face at the man, who lifted an eyebrow in a silent *Yeah?*

Turning to Terri, Kevin smiled big at her, revealing a twin pair of cutie-pie dimples that she had always thought adorable. He was enjoying the moment, as was she.

Second toss was a miss, whizzing by the still-standing bottle. Kevin took a breath and exhaled while tossing the last ball from one hand to the other, his eyes steady on his target. He reared his right arm back and let it rip, hitting the bottle dead-square on the top of the neck. The bottle wobbled and wobbled, and finally it fell.

"Yeah!" all four cheered.

Kevin had his hands raised overhead, as though he had scored the winning touchdown in the final seconds of the big game.

"Give me a *K*," Veronica said with lift of her arm. "Give me an *E*," she added with the other arm raised.

Josh and Terri pitched in and spelled out Kevin's name in whooping, laughing voices.

The booth man offered his hand to a shelf and an assortment of figurines.

"Which do you prefer, Terri?" Kevin asked.

Terri scanned the prizes until her eyes settled on a Scottish terrier figurine in a sitting position with a blue ribbon hanging from its neck. It had brown ears that faded to yellow down to the bridge of its nose, but what really caught Terri's attention were the small black circles for eyes that transmitted a certain kindness.

"I'll have the Scotty," Terri said, pointing.

"Perfect choice," the man replied as he handed the figurine to Terri.

They decided to walk to the end of the boardwalk.

"Twenty-Seventh or Twenty-Eighth Street is our destination," Kevin said.

Down a ways, they got past the hubbub and walked four abreast, with little conversation between them, as though soaking in the evening.

By the time they reached the end of the boardwalk, nightfall had arrived. They stood at the railing overlooking the ocean. The stars hung low. A pale moon spilled silver light across the dark ocean. There was no one else around.

It came over Terri that she was at a transitional period in her life. In a couple of years, she and her companions would be going out into the world. She assumed marriage and children for herself and also the others. Kevin would make a fine husband and father—thoughtful, caring, and reliable. She saw herself working a year or two before considering marriage.

Twenty-four seemed like a reasonable age to say "I do" or even possibly twenty-three if she met Mr. Right.

Whoa, Terri said to herself. *There are still two years of college to complete and then find employment.*

"It looks hauntingly beautiful," Veronica said with a lift of her chin toward the black sky aglitter in starlight, casting faint bands of light on the ocean. "There is something unknowing, unworldly, about the night sky that has always appealed to me."

Josh turned to Veronica with a look or, more precisely, an air of discovery of one finding a great treasure, as he said, "The stars are like little holes in the floor of heaven, emitting hints to its secrets."

"Oh," Veronica said, "that is perfect." She drew out the word *peeer ... feeect* with a look at Josh, indicating it also applied to him.

As they headed back down the boardwalk, Kevin mentioned that tomorrow he and Josh were planning on doing Whiskey Beach in the afternoon followed by the Bottle and Cork.

"We have to work all day Saturday," Terri said. "It will be the busiest day of the year at the pool."

"Bummer," Josh said. "I hear Whiskey Beach is not to be missed."

Terri and Veronica had never been to Whiskey Beach, where alcohol was allowed on an unpatrolled beach. Terri had heard that Saturday afternoons could get uproariously wild there, one big outdoor beer bash.

They were back into the crowded part of the boardwalk, and with it, the magic of the evening faded away.

"We could do something later tomorrow," Kevin suggested.

Terri thought by that point both guys would be pretty wasted from all day on the beach and the ruckus at the Bottle and Cork. "Maybe," she said in a tone that indicated *doubtful.*

On the ride back, they agreed to meet on the Bethany Beach boardwalk at seven the next evening.

"We'll be there," Josh said from the back seat. He laughed. "Not sure if we'll be standing or not, but we'll be there."

Fate comes knocking
Early in the game
To present its wares
Under a false name

Terri awoke at seven on Saturday morning and slipped into a T-shirt and shorts. Last night she had begun reading the Lincoln biography in bed. When she was younger, she used to read for pleasure such stories as *The Outsiders*, *Wizard of Earthsea*, and her favorite, *The Island of Blue Dolphins*, a book based on a true story about a Native American girl stranded on an island for eighteen years. At the end of the book, fate plays a hand as the girl realizes that if not for being stranded, she would not have survived, as her people had all died in a tragic incident—and that, in one's life, adjustments are necessary to adapt to the changing world.

In college, Terri had stopped reading for pleasure. With all the reading assignments and studying required, she used her limited free time in social settings: going to frat and dorm parties, playing hearts in her dorm, or taking in a movie. But she told herself that after graduation she would look into current fiction and biographies.

Terri wanted to dig further into the Lincoln book before work, where it would be all hands on deck for the next three days. Warm, sunny weather was forecast for the extended weekend with the Fourth coming on Monday, so a large turnout was expected at the pool.

With her parents still asleep, Terri, with book in hand, walked softly on the creaky hallway floor out to the porch and sat on a cushy two-seat sofa. The purple martin house was unusually quiet other than a few peeps coming out of the tiny holes to the compartments.

Terri peered closely at the birdhouse. A black snake was winding its way up the pole. She slid open the screen door, grabbed a rake from the shed at the rear of the house, and made a beeline for the birdhouse. The snake's head was near the top of the pole. Terri reached up and positioned the handle end of the rake between the middle of the snake's body and the pole. She jerked the rake away, and the snake's upper half pulled off from the pole, but it sprang itself back on. It was surprisingly strong.

After three more attempts, Terri finally separated the black viper from the metal pole, bringing it down into the grass. Not sure whether the snake was poisonous, she dropped the rake and ran back to the safety of the porch steps. The snake lay motionless for a moment and then slithered away.

Certain that the snake was gone, Terri returned to the shed and found a roll of wire netting, ball of string, tin snips, hammer, and two garden stakes four feet in length. She hammered the stakes into the ground, across from each other at the base of the birdhouse pole. She then cut off a section of wire netting with the tin snips, wrapped it four times around the stakes, and secured the netting to the stakes at the top and bottom with the string.

By the time Terri had returned the tools to the shed and sat back down on the porch, the purple martins were back, coming to and fro as though nothing nearly ruinous to their lives had occurred.

Terri opened the Lincoln book, but she needed a moment. During the rescue, it felt as if she had been fueled by some heroic power to save the martins. But now a sense of fragility had crept into her being. What if the snake had sprung at her? What if it had bitten her?

It's over and done with, she thought as a new feeling came over her, disappointment in not being able to spend the day with Kevin.

It had been such an enjoyable time last night. It was not boisterous, let-it-rip fun, but more an easy comfort. They seemed to fit perfectly together, like two peas in a pod. Kevin didn't have the glamorous looks of Matt, but what he did have was a true-blue persona.

Matt now seemed so like a phase she had gone through, possibly a necessary stage, a life experience where she learned about trust and friendship and also herself. Don't judge a book by its cover or, in this case, a guy by his looks. They can be deceiving, dangerously so.

Last night, Matt must have wondered when neither she nor Veronica had showed up for the party at the guard house. He may well have ended up with Brittany, the blonde umbrella girl. Terri envisioned them in one of the *bang-bang* rooms in bed, naked and entwined, as Brittany assisted Matt in pushing their relationship to a *more personal place*.

Matt wasn't a bad guy. His looks made it difficult to remain faithful in a place like Bethany Beach in the summertime. All around him at work and at play were nubile young women wearing little clothing. She now wondered if he hadn't strayed over their time together.

Anyway, Terri thought, *Matt seems so in my past.* She opened the book to chapter 6 of the Lincoln biography, titled "Without Contemplating Consequences."

By nine thirty, Terri was in her guard suit and matching T-shirt, riding her bike the short distance to the pool. Two cars were in the pool parking lot: Greg's and a white sedan with a Sussex County emblem on the door, which she knew belonged to the inspector from the health department.

Something must be up, she thought as she approached the pool where Greg and the inspector were reading a chlorine test tube filled with water.

The inspector was in his late thirties, with a no-nonsense aura about him. He was a wiry man with light brown hair that he wore in a crew cut. He came across as a by-the-book type who would never cut anyone a break.

"Chlorine residual is way over the limit." The inspector tilted his aviator sunglasses atop his head, his eyes the iciest blue. "I bet the problem is the peristaltic pump." He nodded as if to confirm his words and then motioned for Greg, whose face had blanched as though he were suddenly ill, to follow.

By the time Veronica and Billy arrived, fifteen minutes before opening, the inspector had closed the pool for the day.

"I'll be back tomorrow morning to check on the chlorine level. Until then this pool is closed," the inspector said to a shocked Greg.

"Can't you come back? In a couple of hours, I will have repaired the pump by then and brought the chlorine back to a safe level."

They—Greg, Billy, Veronica, Terri, and the inspector with his aviators firmly secured in place—were on the pool deck.

"No can do," the inspector said, hands on hips and elbows directed outward. He then dropped his hands, turned, and walked away.

"Oh my God," Greg replied in a raised fretful voice. "The board is going to kill me." He was referring to the Bethany West Board of Directors.

"I'll help you in the pump room," Terri said to Greg.

"No," Greg told her in a defeated voice. "I'd rather do it by myself."

"It's not your fault, Greg," Billy said.

Greg shrugged. "See everyone tomorrow."

Teri and Veronica looked at each other as they both seemed to realize at the same time what had just happened. They could do Whiskey Beach and the Bottle and Cork with Kevin and Josh.

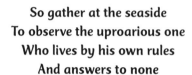

**So gather at the seaside
To observe the uproarious one
Who lives by his own rules
And answers to none**

"Let's ride our bikes to Indian River Inlet and see if we can find Josh and Kevin," Veronica said to Terri at the swimming pool bike rack.

"We'd be looking for a needle in a haystack." Terri shrugged. "If necessary, we'll ride all the way to Whiskey Beach." She pulled her bike back from the rack and swung her leg over to the riding position, one foot on the ground and the other on a pedal. "Let's pack a change of clothes. Put on our beach bathing suits to prepare for a day of fun in the sun, and I'll meet you at your house in fifteen."

She made a face. *Whadda you think?*

"I'm in," Veronica said. "All the way."

By the time Terri got home, her parents had already left to join Irv Hudson and his wife on Irv's motorboat for a day of puttering around the bay and docking for lunch at a restaurant on the water. Terri left a note in the kitchen for her mother and then went to her room to change.

She slipped out of her lifeguard suit and into a light blue one-piece bathing suit that she had purchased last summer. It was the same suit she had worn when she had first met Kevin last year and also Matt this year. She then put on a sea-green T-shirt over the swimsuit.

Rummaging through a dresser drawer, Terri decided on an ivory-colored short-sleeved smock shirt embroidered in bright flowers to wear at the Bottle and Cork. She hadn't worn it since last summer on a date with Kevin. He had called it her flower-girl shirt. She then packed a beach towel, a pair of jean shorts—in which she stowed a pair of undies in the pocket—and the smock shirt into a tote bag.

Terri and Veronica rode their bikes down Collins Avenue, crossed Kent Avenue on foot, headed south for a block before turning left onto Wellington Parkway, went down another block, and made their way to Route 1, where they walked their bikes across the crosswalk of the divided highway. It was a rather roundabout way, though the safest. Bicycle riders were hit by cars every year by distracted vacationers on Garfield Parkway, the main route into town, but the bike lane was narrow and the traffic heavy during the summer months.

On both sides, Route 1 had a wide swath of asphalt designated for bikers and pedestrians. They began pedaling side by side, heading north into a stiff breeze. Their destination was at the base of the Indian River Inlet Bridge, located five miles north of Bethany Beach, five miles south of Dewey Beach proper, and seven miles south of Whiskey Beach.

Terri and Veronica had camped in tents at Indian River Inlet for a weekend after high school graduation with two other girls. It was fun for two days, but some kids they met were tenting there for the summer to save money while working summer jobs—not their idea of a fun summer.

At Garfield Parkway, Terri and Veronica waited for the light to turn green. To their right at the town entrance, situated on a grassy patch of the road verge, was a twenty-four-foot-tall totem pole that had been installed last year. Carved in the middle of symbolic emblems was the face of an Indian, his elongated features accentuated by a proud aquiline nose that hooked down to a sharp tip, heart-shaped lips slightly open as though pondering, and shuttered eyes that had etch marks below, which Terri interpreted as tears. She had learned in an American history class last semester that totem poles represented mythical and historical incidents and were oftentimes a welcome sign for visitors, which Terri found so appropriate for her summer residence.

A half mile north of the town entrance, they passed Fred Hudson Boulevard, which Terri had learned from her father was named after the father of his friend, Irv Hudson.

"Just remember," Veronica said as she pulled behind Terri's bike to allow two women walkers, coming toward them, room to pass. She came back alongside Terri and finished her thought. "Riding into this wind is nothing compared to suicide sprints at Kenwood."

Terri never had minded physical exertion, along with Veronica. It was a part of her friend she had always admired. Other parts she had never dwelled on until the other day at the pool when Veronica intimated something had occurred between her and Matt. That was something she still couldn't dismiss, even though they both—

"Look out, Terri!" Veronica shouted as she moved far right, with Terri on her left, as a pair of preteen boys on souped-up low riders with high handlebars, long curved seats, and bright red chrome were suddenly bearing down upon them, going the wrong way.

Terri veered sharply behind Veronica's bike, almost losing her balance and crashing into a drainage ditch that ran parallel to the road, but she righted herself as they continued north. *Stop daydreaming and pay attention*, Terri told herself as she pulled back up alongside Veronica.

"Idiots!" Veronica screamed over her shoulders.

It was a strenuous workout. *At least a half hour*, Terri thought. They were riding into that dogged wind the entire way to the campground, which was situated across Route 1 from the ocean and on a peninsula jutting into the Indian River Bay. They secured their bikes on a bike rack between the grounds and the parking lot.

"Let's walk around and check on the tents and see if we can find that needle in a haystack," Terri said.

"I hope so," Veronica replied through a deep breath. "Having to ride all the way to Whiskey Beach in that wind might be suicide."

The campground was teeming with rows of tents. The parking lot was packed with RVs, cars, and pickups, some with trailers attached. People were coming and going from a shower facility under a gazebo-like structure; others were on the water in canoes, kayaks, and motorboats. There was not only a permeable hum of activity from the rumbling boat engines and excited voices at the onset of a three-day holiday but also a palatable current of vitality in the air as though they had entered a magnetic force field.

As they began searching along the perimeter, Veronica said, "I just remembered. Josh told me they were staying in a green tent."

"Yeah," Terri added, "Kevin said it was an old Boy Scouts tent of his."

They had reached the end and turned back down a row, passing a man wearing a floppy canvas hat with fishing lures attached to the short brim. He was holding a tackle box in one hand and fishing pole in the other.

"Ladies," the man said with a tone that said, *Seize the day.*

Halfway down the third row, they came to an olive-green tepee tent. Stitched into the side was an emblem of a standing eagle, wings and tail feathers spread, with a stars-and-stripes shield on its chest.

"That's the Boy Scouts emblem," Terri said.

Veronica asked, "Josh, you in there?"

Silence. She opened the door flap, and they found two sleeping bags; a pair of grocery bags packed with T-shirts, underwear, socks, and towels; and a red, dinged, and dented cooler.

Veronica checked the cooler. "Only one lonely green bottle of beer in need of company," she said to Terri. "This has to be them."

"Bet they went to make a beer and ice run," Terri told her.

Fifteen minutes later, Kevin and Josh showed up with a case of beer and a ten-pound bag of ice.

"Whoa," Josh said. "Whiskey Beach anyone."

"Hey," Kevin said through a big grin to Terri. He placed down the case of beer. "Hope you girls like Rolling Rock ponies."

"Love 'em," Veronica said, throwing a *we're-gonna-have-us-some-fun* look at Josh.

"How did y'all get here?" Kevin asked.

"Bikes," Terri told him.

"Wow," Kevin said with a lift of his eyebrows to add credence to his words. "I'm impressed."

"Hungry?" Josh questioned with an inquiring glint to Veronica.

"Famished," she said. "Riding against the wind can do that to a girl."

After lunch at a family restaurant in Rehoboth Beach, they drove the short distance to the Whiskey Beach parking lot.

A park ranger in a khaki uniform and Smokey the Bear hat pointed Kevin to a parking spot at the rear of the half-full lot, past which was a gable-framed wooden structure with his and hers bathrooms.

Kevin and Josh lifted the cooler out of the trunk, a handle at each end. The girls carried their tote bags and the boys' towels. They came to the edge of the beach. The guys put down the cooler, all four surveying the scene before them.

"What would you have done," Kevin asked Terri, "if you hadn't found us back at Indian River?"

"We'd have showed up here tired, but we would have showed."

Kevin shot a glance at Terri. A small smile crinkled in the corner of his eyes before returning his attention to the beach.

There was something wild and free about what lay before them. The beach was an expanse of windswept shoreline. To their immediate left was a dune of reedy grass, and farther down were two masonry towers at least fifty feet high, with two horizontal openings near the top, below which were smaller vertical ones.

"They look like concrete silos," Terri said.

"Looks can be deceiving," Kevin told her. "They were World War II watchtowers for German subs."

"No way," Josh said as he peered out at the ocean as though trying to envision a German U-boat emerging above the surface. He then turned back to Kevin. "I had no idea the Germans were this close to American soil during the war."

"A cook at the restaurant I worked at last year in Ocean View was an army tower observer during the war," Kevin said with a lift of his chin toward the towers. "Not only to watch for subs but for spies trying to disembark. German subterfuge."

The crowd was mostly in their early twenties: girls sunbathing on towels or blankets, a few groups of guys and girls, and then the predominant gathering of guys all drinking beer and all checking out the girls. There were young people all around them, but the beach was so wide and long that there was plenty of space to situate about halfway between the dunes and the water.

"Let's get us some rays," Kevin said as he removed his T-shirt. His body was surprisingly lean and muscular, and he was as tan as an ocean lifeguard.

Terri had noticed that he had seemed more toned by his arms that were leaner and tauter, but his chest and torso were similar to what she would expect on a beach guard. *Nice*, Terri thought. *Very nice.*

"Kevin," Terri said, "I never asked you what kind of work you are doing this summer."

"Laborer on a concrete crew."

"Really?" Terri asked. "What exactly do you do?"

"Jackhammer out driveways, hoist the chunks of broken concrete on the truck, set forms, grade and spread gravel with rakes, and roll out and cut wire mesh. Then the concrete mixer truck arrives, and we spread the concrete with come-alongs and finish it with hand floats and trowels."

"Really?" Terri said before laughing. "I have to stop saying *really*."

"It's déjà vu," Kevin told her.

"So it is," Terri said.

Josh, on the other hand, had a light tan on his arms and legs, but his lanky, lean upper body was lily white.

"You need sunscreen, Josh." Veronica reached in her beach bag and removed a tube of Coppertone.

Josh spread his arms out. "I am all yours, fair maiden. Have your way with this neglected yank of manhood."

Kevin broke out into hooting, hands-on-knees laughter. "Oh, Josh," he said as he straightened back up. "To thy own self be true."

"You too, Mr. Tan Concrete Man," Terri replied in a singsongy voice. She offered her hand to Veronica, who squeezed a healthy dab of sunscreen into Terri's palm.

"Not only a rare and radiant maiden," Kevin said with an uptick in his voice, "but with a penchant for instant poetry. Who knew?"

"And unlike some people," Terri added as she began to apply the ointment on Kevin's back, "my poetry is original. Mr. Poe."

After the girls finished applying sunscreen to the guys, Josh looked over his shoulder at Veronica. "Turnabout is fair play."

"Oh, Mr. Congressman," Veronica said in a mock breathy voice, "I thought you would never ask."

"Ah then, Miss Monroe," Josh said through a mischievous grin, "would you whisper sweet nothings to me while I complete my fair play?"

"Possibly later on. When you are addressed as Mr. President, I will sing to you on your birthday." Veronica's eyes then brightened. "Make that very possibly."

After everyone had been sun-proofed, they set up their towels on the beach but remained standing, as did most of the various groups of kids around them. Only a few girls were still sunbathing.

It seemed this was a place to stand and take in the clear blue sky and the rolling tide pounding the beach. It was a place to see and be seen and to bask in a certain hospitable warmth transmitted among this gathering of youth. And along with this friendly youthful vibe were the anticipatory voices of a good time a coming, all seemingly working in conjunction to create a sensation so very sweet, an experience Terri had never felt before.

Josh pointed to a group of a half-dozen portly guys. "Look at them," he said in an appreciative tone of awe and wonder. "Beer barrel polka, anyone?"

The group had a sixteen-gallon keg in a steel utility tub packed in ice. A wooden pole that was secured to the rim of the keg fluttered a skull and crossbones flag with *Rally Crew* scrolled across the top.

"Now that," Josh said with a bemused, appreciative smile, "is a party-hearty lot."

"Ah, yes." Kevin grinned. "They are the Rally Crew and … Ta-da!" he said with a sweeping gesture of his hand. "Here comes their leader, the intrepid Black Bart."

Approaching the Rally Crew, to hooting cheers, was a tall, barrel-chested throwback in his mid-thirties with a long face and large dark thunderclap eyes that were slightly protruding and hinting at intelligence. He was wearing a black T-shirt and olive-green cargo shorts.

"I met Black Bart last summer at the Cork," Kevin said with a remembering glimmer in his eyes. "He is the king of Dewey Beach."

"He looks like a scallywag king," Terri added.

"And then some," Kevin said in a spirited tone. "The *Washington Post* did an article last summer about Dewey Beach, and Black Bart had a line I will never forget. 'You check your brains in when you cross the Bay Bridge, and you pick them up on the way home.' He's like the Pied Piper of Dewey Beach. Everybody loves Black Bart."

"Ice-cold pony anyone?" Josh dipped his hand into the cooler packed with ice and seven-ounce green bottles of Rolling Rock.

"Yes," Veronica said. "We need to get into the spirit of Whiskey Beach."

Josh popped open a beer with a can opener tied to a handle on the cooler and handed it to Veronica, who smiled a thank-you. "If I may paraphrase a line from Rick Blaine—"

"Who is Rick Blaine?" Veronica asked, shielding her eyes from the bright sun as she squinted at Josh.

Josh lifted his finger to indicate patience. He popped open another beer and handed it to Terri and then two more so that all four held beers. He raised his bottle. "I think this is the beginning of a beautiful day of friendship and comity."

"Hear! Hear! To friendship and comity," Kevin said as all four clinked bottles.

"Aha." Veronica said. "Humphrey Bogart in *Casablanca.*"

"Great movie." Josh affirmed with a confirming nod. "Though with a bittersweet ending."

The ponies went down surprisingly quick, and before Terri knew it, her bottle, as well as the others, were empty.

"Look," Josh said as he offered his hand to a group of big athletic-looking guys in their mid-twenties, "they're drinking silver bullets."

"Silver bullets?" Veronica asked.

"Coors beer. Rocky Mountain brewed beer. The best dang beer in the world."

"Would you like for me to get us a round?" Veronica asked.

"Absolutely," Josh answered.

"Mr. Congressman," Veronica said, "four ponies, kind sir."

With two bottles in each hand, Veronica sauntered on over in her one-piece dark green swimsuit with thin crossing straps in the low scoop back that revealed a tantalizing indentation down the middle of her bare back. It appeared as though her perfectly constructed body fit the suit as though made specifically for her.

Kevin, Josh, and Terri watched silently as Veronica smiled big while offering the bottles of Rolling Rock. There were five guys in all, and all possessed that quintessential look of a young professional, but still there remained a glimmer and glint in their eyes suggesting a desire to hold on a tad longer to their glorious youth.

Veronica had positioned herself so that her side was facing Terri's group, obviously wanting to present a clear view of her upcoming performance. As Veronica presented her case, accompanied by a nod over her shoulder toward Terri's group, a confident it-is-in-the-bag grin hovered about her lips.

She's good, Terri thought to herself. *Very good when the mood strikes her.*

One fellow in the group stowed the Rolling Rocks in their huge cooler, pulled out four Coors, and lifted his chin toward Terri's group. With that, he walked back over with Veronica, who chatted up to him, her expression that of gracious recipient.

Veronica said to the group, "This is Patrick ... Patrick ..."

"McHady," the young man replied. "We have plenty of Coors." He nimbly offered Terri a beer with two fingers while clutching in his palm the other can.

"Where did you get them?" Josh asked as he took a Coors. "It isn't sold east of the Mississippi."

"I just transferred back from Boulder," Patrick said as he handed a beer to Kevin, "and stocked my Fiat Spider with seven cases on the drive back." He smiled a dimpled grin as if mostly to himself. "Hardly room for anything else." He stood over six feet tall with broad shoulders and had a ruggedly handsome face of a daring-do adventurer.

"Veronica," Patrick said with a tilt of his head toward her standing next to him, "was hard to say no to." He handed Veronica the last beer and then lifted his hand farewell and turned, walking back to his friends.

"Well," Kevin added as he lifted the pop-top, "let's drink us some Coors." He took a sip, smacked his lips, and then swallowed. "Man," he said with meaning, "that is great beer."

And Terri had to agree. "Besides being ice cold," she said, holding up the mellow-yellow and golden-colored can with swirly dark blue fonts that read *Coors*, "it tastes like frosted flakes with a fizz." She took another taste. "Wow, that is really, really good."

Josh looked over at Veronica. "Thank you, fair lady, for this perfect libation in this perfect location."

"It 'twas nothing, good sir," Veronica said with a lifting of her beer. "Just me being me."

As the afternoon progressed, the groups began to mingle. Guys approached girls, offering beer, though not the Coors group, who had other girls approach and ask for beers, all of whom they gladly supplied.

Some of the younger guys got so drunk that they passed out on their towels. One was a skinny redheaded kid, dead to the world, spread-eagle on a blanket. His ghostly white skin was flecked with tiny freckles. He looked like Howdy Doody on a bender. Terri went over, tucked his arms into his side, and covered him in a towel.

When she returned, Kevin mocked applause. "Betsy Ross to the rescue," he said, smiling. But in his eyes was a glint of recognizing a good deed done.

Terri turned to the sudden cacophonous sounds of a banging drum and off-key fiddles.

Good Lord! It was Black Bart parading down the beach with the Rally Crew in tow. One portly fellow directly behind Black Bart was banging a drumstick for all it was worth on a snare drum hanging from a strap on his neck. Two others, walking shoulder to shoulder, were playing or, better stated, blowing into wooden fifes behind them. Two lads were marching with exaggerated exuberance of pumping arms with elbows locked while high-stepping their merry way along, all of them like ragtag boy soldiers behind the gargantuan Black Bart.

Wearing an American flag bandana around his head, Black Bart halted in front of a pair of middle-aged women sitting in beach chairs under an umbrella. One was slender; the other was heavyset. Age-wise and dress-wise, they looked out of place, dressed in long-sleeved blouses and beach pants and broad-brimmed sunhats made of straw.

Black Bart raised his hand for the band to stop playing. "Ladies," he said in a raspy growl that seemed to have been extensively primed by strong tobacco and alcohol. He placed his forearm across his waist and bowed in an exaggerated manner. "May my musically challenged colleagues and I perform a patriotic rendition for you?"

"We'd be honored, darling," the heavyset woman said. There was a country twang to her voice.

Black Bart touched the toes of his right foot into the sand and pivoted precisely one hundred and eighty degrees to his right on his left heel. Eyeing his motley crew, Black Bart crossed his arms in front of himself. "No instruments, lads. We are going to sing a cappella on my instruction."

He did another about-face and raised a finger overhead, and Black Bart and his Rally mates began singing "God Bless America." The two women smiled big at Black Bart. They were enjoying this moment.

Like a locomotive engine picking up steam, Black Bart was now belting it out in a deep, melodious voice, the raspy rough edges seemingly swept away by a sudden gentle sea breeze.

> God bless America
> Land that I love
> Stand beside her
> And guide her
> Through the night with the light from above

People were gathering around Black Bart and his Rally Crew in a semicircle, including Terri's group. The big man raised his hands, indicating for everyone to join in. Arms over shoulders, everyone sang as one voice.

> From the mountains
> To the prairies
> To the oceans
> White with foam
> God bless America
> My home sweet home

At the conclusion of the song, Black Bart presented another bow to the two ladies.

"Thank you." they shouted at Black Bart. They extended their hands out to the other singers and offered another thank-you.

"Honey pie," the slender woman said in a soft, appreciative voice, "who are you?"

"Black Bart at your service, ma'am."

"Of course you are," the heavyset woman replied. "You just made our day … Black Bart."

Black Bart straightened, offered a crooked left-handed salute to the ladies, and pivoted on his left heel, turning another of his flawless about-faces. "Rally Crew," he growled out, "muster at the keg."

Terri was having a blast, amazed at the freedom of it all. Kids were drinking, shouting, laughing, and having a grand old time. There was not a bit of macho posturing from any of the guys, some who looked like college athletes with their bulging muscles and thick necks. One group of jocks was back along the dunes, tossing a football around. It was as though everyone seemed to appreciate the freedom allotted to drink alcohol in public, many of whom were underage, including Terri.

"Hey, Black Bart." Kevin shouted toward the Rally Crew, where the big man was standing at their keg, a shit-eating grin on his face as he took it all in.

His mates seemed to be regaling in old exploits from bygone years—talking, shouting, and screaming over one another. Black Bart turned and looked over, searching for the location of Kevin's voice.

Kevin lifted his hand. "I met you last year at the Cork."

"Of course you did," Black Bart said with a conspiratorially wink. "And I expect you and your mateys to be there this afternoon." He lifted a finger as though to say, *Don't forget.*

Black Bart turned back to his Rally Crew and offered an inaudible bon mot to the conversation. The Rally Crew broke into uproarious laughter with heads thrown back and beer bellies jiggling.

"Wouldn't miss it for the world," Kevin said in a sotto voice. He turned to Terri. "Would we?"

Hootenanny, pootenanny
Twiddly dee
We're gonna party
Til we can no longer see

On the way to the Bottle and Cork, Kevin asked if they wanted to stop at a diner and get something to eat.

"Yes," Veronica said from the back seat.

"Me too," Terri added.

"Josh?" Kevin asked with a tilt of his head toward the back seat. "Are you still with us?"

"Roger … Wilco … Captain … Kevin," Josh said in a slurred voice, each word dragged out.

Josh had drunk one Coors and five ponies on the beach, not a huge amount, a little less than four twelve-ounce beers, but this all seemed like a new experience to him. The social aspect of outdoor drinking in the sun, and with a contagiously social group like the Rally Crew, it seemed to have let something loose in Josh.

He was like an amateur archeologist on expedition who, upon having discovered Whiskey Beach and its denizens, found it all had been a bit overwhelming. Kevin had told Terri that Josh wasn't a big drinker, more of a social observer at college parties.

Kevin turned on a side road a couple of blocks from the Bottle and Cork. On his left was a shack-like joint with a neon sign over the double-door entrance, *Theo's Diner.* Terri pointed to a car leaving a parking spot, and Kevin zipped up and backed right in with eyes on the rearview mirror.

"Nice job." Terri then turned her head to the back seat and saw Josh fast asleep, his head resting on Veronica's shoulder.

"You guys go in and eat and then bring something out for us," Veronica said.

How different Veronica looked, though not her beauty, which was constant. It was as if a new expression had been added to her repertoire, one of modest understanding, as though she was perfectly content to spend the rest of the day in the back seat with the passed-out Josh.

Opposites do attract, Terri thought as she and Kevin exited the car.

It was late afternoon, and many of the diner customers were already under the influence. It was like a loud party that was on the verge of breaking out, but then the food would arrive, and a rowdy table turned quiet as burgers and fries and subs were devoured and washed down by soft drinks with youthful hunger.

Theo's Diner had no wait staff. Food was ordered and paid for at a counter. A numbered ticket was given to the customer by a man with a five-o'clock shadow and a seen-it-all demeanor, but also accompanied by the look of someone in charge, most likely the owner. He looked Greek with a bump on the bridge of a large, straight nose, thick, dark eyebrows, and a thicket of salt-and-pepper hair that at one time must have been coal black. He looked like a Theo and also sounded like one as he shouted out orders ready for pickup.

"Number seventy-seven," he said, emphasizing the end of each word so that it came out "Numb-er seven-tee sev-enn.

Behind the counter was the kitchen, where a line of young people, who had that hard-knock look about them, were cooking up a storm on a line of griddles and fryers.

Kevin and Terri slipped into a booth, with Kevin holding their order on a tray and Terri a carryout bag for Josh and Veronica.

"The old vet I worked with last year told me—" Kevin paused as an uproar of laughter and table pounding came from the booth behind them. As he unwrapped his steak-and-cheese sub packed tightly in butcher paper, he continued, "That Whiskey Beach got its name when he and his fellow soldiers stationed here during the war would go there to drink and party without having to worry about getting hassled by the police."

"Makes sense … the name, that is," Terri said as she took a hearty bite into her cold cut submarine before turning to the sound of breaking glass.

A busboy with a broom and dustpan was hustling over to a booth of four college-aged boys, two of whom were straining in an intense arm wrestling competition. On the floor was the shattered glass, a victim of these young gladiators. Terri had noticed them on Whiskey Beach, the muscular group tossing around a football.

"Look," Kevin said, looking over Terri's shoulder.

Off Terri's left, coming down the aisle barefoot, wearing a bathing suit and white undershirt, was Howdy Doody from Whiskey Beach, the passed-out boy who Terri had covered with a towel. His face and neck were beet-red, as were his calves and ankles, in stark contrast to his arms and thighs, which had only a light pink hue.

He was with two friends. All three appeared no more than eighteen, probably just graduated from high school. They placed their trays down at the booth across the aisle from Terri and Kevin and took a seat, Howdy on the outside across from Terri.

Howdy took a deep breath and then grimaced as he lightly put his hand on his cheek. "I'm on fire." His expression was that of one enduring a difficult day, but still not wanting to give up on it.

"You needed a bigger towel," Kevin said in a low voice to Terri as he cut his sub down the middle with a plastic fork, oozing melted cheese onto the butcher paper.

"Well," Terri replied as she opened a packet of ketchup and squirted it on their order of french fries, "imagine where he'd be if I hadn't covered him."

Back at the car, Terri and Kevin found Veronica and Josh kissing. It wasn't an all-out go-for-it make-out session, but more of a gentle isn't-this-wonderful outing. Their fingers were interlaced, resting on Josh's thigh. Both were lost in this moment of amorous bliss.

Kevin and Terri got inside the car, banging the doors shut, which finally broke up the lovebirds.

"I see my first lieutenant has rallied for duty." Kevin handed the carryout bag of food back to Josh.

"Never felt better, Sergeant Major," Josh said as he dug into the bag and handed Veronica a napkin and a hamburger wrapped in a thin sheet of wax paper. He placed a carton paper bag of fries between them and then unraveled his hamburger.

"And after I eat this epicurean's delight—" he said before taking a chomp out of his burger, with ketchup leaking onto his chin.

Veronica dabbed her napkin on his chin. "You'll be ready for come what may," she added, completing his sentence.

"Exactly, my dear," Josh said through an exaggerated, lopsided smile.

Kevin looked at Terri and shook his head. He then returned his gaze to the back seat. "Whatever is going on with Mr. Peepers?"

After a few laps around the Bottle and Cork gravel parking lot, Kevin found an opening down at the end, a stone's throw from Rehoboth Bay. Before departing Whiskey Beach, all four had used the restrooms to change into shorts and T-shirts, the girls in their flip-flops and Kevin and Josh in sneakers. Terri had decided not to wear her flower-girl shirt, instead staying with the sea-green T-shirt. She wasn't sure why, other than a sense that she should save it for another time and another place.

Upon exiting the car, the thumping beat of music permeated the air.

"That's coming from the outdoor patio." Kevin gestured to an L-shaped, ten-foot faded turquoise masonry wall, one side of which ran parallel to the parking lot. "That's where we want to be."

They entered the open-air entrance. To their left, a canvas barrier met the end of the masonry wall, enclosing the patio. Shouts and laughter competed with the blaring blast of rock and roll rising up and out into the summertime air.

As they waited in line, all four got out their IDs to present to a bouncer, a big, burly type in his early thirties with olive-brown skin and a round, smooth face—Samoan ancestry perhaps—who was sitting on a stool. He was checking IDs on some. For others, he let pass with a hand motioning them through. To the bouncer's rear was the indoor section with a large circular bar.

As they moved up the line, approaching the end of the canvas barrier, Terri heard the rapid chatter of the DJ talking up a wet T-shirt contest, as the decrescendo chorus of "Back Stabbers" by the O'Jays drifted away.

> They smile in your face
> All the time they want to take your place
> The back stabbers (back stabbers)

Josh was the only one of legal age, having just turned twenty-one. He showed his driver's license and was waved through. He had Veronica at his side, smiling big at the bouncer, whose no-nonsense countenance broke momentarily as he grinned back at the beautiful young woman before him. She walked right in, slipping her fake ID into her back pocket as she passed.

Kevin handed his ID over for inspection.

"No good, man," the bouncer said. He waved to a group of older guys to enter.

As they passed, Kevin asked, "What's the problem?"

The bouncer dabbed his finger on the photo. "This don't even look like you, bro." He handed it back. "You're lucky I don't tear it up."

"Big Ray," a voice boomed from seemingly out of nowhere.

The bouncer looked over his shoulder to the indoor bar, where shouldering his way through the swell of people came Black Bart to the rescue.

"Ray … moond," Black Bart growled in a tone ringing with camaraderie. "I'd consider it a personal favor if you would authorize the entrance of my two young friends." He wrapped his arm around Big Ray's shoulder and gave it a squeeze. Black Bart then leaned back and offered the same conspiratorial wink to the bouncer that he had to Kevin at Whiskey Beach.

Big Ray looked at Black Bart and then Kevin, and lifted his chin for them to enter. Kevin raised his hand to Black Bart, who nodded *No problem* before returning into the thicket of patrons at the indoor bar.

The spirited atmosphere of the outdoor patio was like an extension of Whiskey Beach, but ratcheted up by the enclosed space. In the middle of which sprouted a birch tree with a long, narrow trunk, its sparse foliage looming over a gable roof gazebo serving bar, with two quick-moving and lickety-split-mixing bartenders wearing shorts and T-shirts.

The place was packed, with nary a chair on the premises. People were standing in clustered groups, shouting over the blare of "Touch Me, Babe" by the Doors.

Yeah! Come on, come on, come on, come on
Now touch me, babe
Can't you see that I am not afraid?
What was that promise that you made?

The DJ was situated on a raised platform that ran alongside the canvas barrier. He was seated in front of a horizontal table supporting two turntables and other electronic apparatus with wires running to wall speakers strategically placed around the patio walls. He was peering over his equipment, talking to a woman in a G-string bikini, partially covered by a see-through mesh sleeveless shirt.

The woman, appearing to be in her late twenties, had the look of porn queen—bombshell body with generous breasts, a taut torso, and perfectly shaped legs with subtle recesses and curves at the knee and ankle. But what gave Terri the inclination toward porn was her striking face that hinted at wanton pleasure. And also her voice had a sexy rasp, indicating a different set of priorities.

"Joe Bock is the DJ," Kevin said. "He's a riot."

Veronica and Josh approached, sidestepping their way through the mob of people, each with a plastic cup of beer.

"This place is so amazing," Josh said through a wide-eyed grin.

Kevin told Terri to wait and he would get them beers. While he was gone, Terri stood off to the side of the DJ platform with Josh and Veronica, taking in the spectacle before them. The noise level was unbelievable, raucous voices merging into a singular uproar penetrated by barks of laughter and blasted over by the thumping music.

While the music played, Joe Bock was talking smack to a group of guys with military haircuts and a swagger to them. *Marines*, Terri thought.

Back and forth the marines exchanged insults with Joe Bock, who was in his late twenties. He was around six feet tall with dark features, a receding hairline, and perceptive eyes that smiled naughty boy. The marines were telling him how ugly and fat he was in that competitive-macho-guy animated manner.

"Me!" Joe Bock said in a gleeful tone. "Youse four jarheads are so ugly, when yo' mamas dropped youse off at school, they all got a ticket for littering."

The amazing thing about this encounter was that no one was paying a bit of attention to it. Guys were eyeing girls and vice versa; groups of couples were wrapped in loud conversations, shouting out to each other. Everyone was laughing and talking over the conversation and having what appeared to be the time of their lives.

Halfway through Terri's first beer, Joe Bock started to introduce the first contestant for the wet T-shirt contest when screeching audio feedback interrupted him. He sat back for a moment and tried again.

"That's my PA system telling me to *shaddup* and get the first young lady up on stage." He called out the name of the first contestant.

A girl who was wearing cutoffs and a white T-shirt, cut to expose her midriff, raised her hand and shouted, "That's me." She was a tall, long-legged blonde who had the look of one acting on a dare, a drunken dare. Blondie stepped up onto the platform space.

Joe Bock motioned her to come closer. He raised a spray bottle and said into his microphone, "Ice cold! No, pain, no gain."

Blondie gasped as the spray hit her chest. Her T-shirt turned translucent, exposing her nipples with areolas the size of silver dollars. Then "I Get Around" by the Beach Boys began playing, and Blondie started gyrating and shaking her fanny while raising her arms over her head as she swayed to the music. Her expression was that of disengaged pleasure, as though she were in her bedroom alone, dancing in front of the mirror.

Guys had gathered up close to get a better view, with the marines in front. At first, they were watching in awed silence, taking in every move.

Then the marines began shouting encouragement, "Yeah, yeah! Go, girl!"

Terri couldn't imagine ever performing like that in front of a crowd of drunken guys. She glanced at Veronica, who had a look of reserved distance, not disapproving but more with detached curiosity. Josh was taking it all in with his wide-eyed look, but not with any carnal lust, but more as an observer enjoying the moment.

Kevin, on the other hand, had a wry smile planted firmly in the corner of his mouth. He seemed to be enjoying the moment, but also there was a glint of sexual attraction. He was a twenty-year-old red-blooded American boy after all.

When Blondie finished, she received a round of applause and shrieking whistles from the guys gathered around the platform. The rest of the people were still huddled in groups, shouting over the din of the contest. Some of the guys were glancing casual peeks at the stage. It seemed they had seen these wet T-shirt contest before. *Been there, done that.*

A couple more girls came up and danced, jiggling and bouncing around. Guys still gathered around, absorbed in the performance.

Then Porn Girl took the stage, whereupon she removed her mesh shirt in increments as though performing a striptease, with tilting shoulders and swaying hips. Muffled *oohs* were gasped by her admirers, as Porn Girl was now practically naked, dressed only in her high heels and purple G-string bikini, her large firm breasts looking to burst out.

She held her shirt overhead with arms extended before lowering one arm out to the side, dangling the shirt to Joe Bock, who, while grinning from ear to ear, took it from her. It reminded Terri of a risqué vaudeville act.

Still holding his grin, Joe Bock index-fingered her over and then sprayed her breasts, drawing another appreciative gasp from the guys standing below the stage, even though nothing further was revealed. It was more of an anticipatory reflex reaction as though imagining the bounty behind the skimpy costume.

Porn Girl began swaying her hips in a slow and seductive manner to the sound of "The Girl Can't Help It" by Little Richard.

> She can't help it, the girl can't help it
> She can't help it, the girl can't help it
> If she walks by and the men folks get engrossed
> She can't help it, the girl can't help it

Porn Girl began to increase her tempo, thrusting and grinding her hips. But then something happened that shocked Terri. The marines started booing.

"Get that bimbo off the stage."

Some of the other guys gathered around the platform joined in. "Get her off, Joe. Amateurs only."

At the end of the performance, Porn Girl extended her arms out to her side, put her left foot behind her right, and curtsied flawlessly in her high heels to a chorus of boos. She then went over to Joe Bock and placed her hand behind his neck, bent down, and planted a kiss smack-dab on his lips.

Joe Bock leaned back in his chair, his eyes screaming, *Yowser!* He then said into the microphone, "That's, ladies and gentlemen, what I'm talkin' about."

Porn Girl then slipped on her mesh shirt and exited the platform, her expression a stone-cold indifference of a starlet receiving a bad review.

"Wow," Josh said, "this is like a movie."

At the conclusion of the contest, Joe Bock had six out of the seven dancers come up on stage individually. Porn Girl didn't show. For each contestant, Joe asked the audience, "Let me hear me it, folks." He then cocked his ear, listening to the decibel level of the cheers. The winner was a curvy brunette, who received twenty-five dollars and a round of applause and whistles.

After the dance competition, the energy level seemed to wane a bit. People were still having a loud and good-old time, but a full day of drinking in the sun and continuing on at the Bottle and Cork was having its effect.

There was a three-foot circular brick wall around the birch tree, and Terri and Veronica took a seat when a couple left while Kevin and Josh went for another round of beers. Terri had consumed four beers for the day. She was feeling a pleasant buzz. Veronica seemed about the same.

Terri glanced over at Kevin waiting in line at the outdoor bar, and when she turned back, she saw Matt and Brittany getting their IDs checked by the bouncer. She looked at Veronica, who appeared indifferent, but Terri felt uncomfortable. She wasn't exactly sure why.

In the mass of people, Matt and Brittany walked right past Terri and Veronica, with Matt unaware. Brittany glanced back and smirked a look at Terri as if to say, *Nah, nah, nah, nah. He's mine, and you can't have him.* She then shot a look at Veronica indicating, *Same for you.* They got in line at the patio bar, a couple of people behind Kevin and Josh.

A guy approached Terri and asked if she would like to dance. It was one of the marines, of average size with a lean and wiry build, his arms knotted with ropy muscle.

"I'm with someone," she said.

"Ah, come on," the marine countered. "Just one dance." He extended his hand to her.

"She said no," Veronica said in a firm voice.

The marine kept his gaze on Terri, his eyes two narrow slits. He grabbed Terri's wrist and tried to get her to stand, but she jerked it out of his grasp.

A large mass of humanity moved in behind the marine. Black Bart leaned over the young man's shoulder and said in a soft but firm voice, "Leave her be, son."

The marine turned and looked up. Black Bart had a stogy secured in the corner of his mouth, his dark brow raised as if to say, *Are we clear?* He wore an expression of carefree confidence, but tinged with it a trace of iron set back deep in his gaze, the drill instructor confronting one of his recruits.

By now, the other three marines had appeared and stood alongside their buddy, eyeing carefully the big man before them. Black Bart stood there, his gaze steady and sure.

Then Big Ray, the bouncer who was nearly the size of Black Bart, came over and said to the marines, "Two choices: walk away now or you will be escorted from the premises." He lifted his chin as if say, *What's it going to be?*

The marines stood there for a moment, looking at Big Ray and Black Bart, two giant men standing shoulder to shoulder.

"Tell you what," Black Bart said in his raspy growl. He drew on his cigar and exhaled a puff of smoke, with one eye squinting at the marines. "What say I buy a round for you fellas at the bar?" He lifted his brow, his eyes saying, *Well?*

The marines looked at each other, and the one who had asked Terri to dance said, "Sounds like a plan, big man."

As Black Bart and the jarheads retreated to the indoor bar, Veronica said to Terri, "The fortress was breached."

"What?"

"I fucked Matt the other night."

Terri's heart tightened. She felt as though her spirit was spiraling away from her corporeal being. To her core, she now understood the word *disloyalty.*

Josh and Kevin came up with their beers.

"What was that all about?" Kevin asked as he handed Terri a cup of beer.

"Black Bart to the rescue," Veronica said.

As Veronica explained what had transpired, Terri tried to gather herself. She had sensed that something had happened between Matt and Veronica, but for her to have gone all the way was a stunner.

"Can't leave you for minute," Kevin said to Terri.

Terri offered Kevin a shrug and a smile. And then coming into her view was Matt and Brittany approaching. Terri and Veronica stood, standing between Kevin and Josh.

"Hey, how is everyone doing?" Matt's tone was that of one attempting good cheer, but mixed in was a tingle of guilty nerves. He flashed a glance at Terri, looked past Veronica, and then offered a hand to Josh, introducing himself.

"We met the other night. Right here," Josh said, shaking Matt's hand.

A look of embarrassed recognition came over Matt before he offered a hand to Kevin. "Good to see you again."

Kevin, his expression noncommittal, kept his hand at his side, and Matt jerked his hand back. After an awkward pause, Brittany, who had her arm wrapped tight around Matt's waist, cleared her throat.

"Sorry," Matt said. "This is my girlfriend, Brittany."

Terri felt her mouth gape before she caught herself. *Who is this guy? And did I really go out with him? And what do I do with Veronica?*

The ride back to the campground was a quiet affair. Josh had quickly picked up that something had transpired that put a damper on the evening, but like a good politician, he had no comment.

Terri wanted time alone with Kevin, maybe a walk and talk back at the campground. Also she wanted to be away from Veronica and her tryst with Matt. Though Terri was curious as to how much Kevin had known about what had transpired with Veronica and Matt. She surmised from Kevin's standoffish behavior toward Matt that he knew that she had been dating Matt and must have witnessed something going down the other night at the Bottle and Cork.

Kevin broke the silence in the car as they drove over the Indian River Inlet Bridge, just a minute from the campground. "Do you girls want to leave your bikes at the grounds and I'll drive you back to Bethany?"

"Not me," Terri said. "I want to talk with you and then ride my bike back before dark."

"Josh can take me and my bike back," Veronica said as the car turned into the campground's entrance.

The campground was quiet. A few folks were cooking on grills, and others were sitting at picnic benches, beers in hand. Terri and Kevin were walking along the bay, letting the day's events settle in before conversing.

"You knew I was dating Matt," Terri said more as a fact than a question.

They stopped walking. Kevin looked out over the bay. Early evening sunlight glittered on the water and brightened the hulls of the boats in the bay. "I figured it out when I overheard one of the guys in Veronica's group the other night at the Cork mention that he wondered if Matt remembered if he was dating Veronica's best friend and not Veronica."

He took her hand, his palm calloused sandpaper rough from his summer employment, but in his touch, she felt his strength and his compassion. At this very moment in time, Terri felt safe and secure.

She looked out at the water. A young couple was paddling a kayak toward shore. They worked in unison, paddling three strokes on the opposite side and then switching. How proper it all looked to Terri, an unoccupied rowboat bobbing gently atop the tranquil water and a light breeze offering a cool respite from the heat of the day. And in the distance, the horizon met the sky in a flush of colors.

"You knew about ..." Terri paused, trying to find the right words.

"I spotted them the other night at the Cork, doing the deed in the back seat of a station wagon."

"It's all pretty crazy." Terri turned to Kevin, her eyes staring into his. *How true and blue he looked*, she thought.

"It worked out in the end." Kevin leaned into her, kissing Terri on the lips.

It felt right to be held in Kevin's arms and kissing him back, to feel his hands pressing into her shoulder blades and hers in his. It felt good for his tongue to find hers, to be lost in the moment with this true-blue guy.

But she needed time to sort through it all. It was time to figure out exactly how she felt about Kevin. Was it a rebound reaction to Matt and Veronica, or was there more?

Terri pulled back from Kevin's embrace. "I better get back before dark."

"I understand," Kevin said. "Ride and think."

"You get me."

Terri pedaled with effort into a stiff breeze. The wind had changed direction. *Grind, grind, grind* was a mantra she used when swimming endless laps during training sessions. Now she thought, *Grind, grind, grind to clear my mind.* Exercise had always been a tool Terri used to bring things into focus.

She thought back to seventh grade and her first day of swim practice at Kenwood during Memorial Day weekend, when Veronica had spotted her in the girls' locker room.

"You're a swimmer?" Veronica had asked as she sized up Terri as though seeing her for the first time.

Terri was at the door, dressed in her brand-new dark blue Kenwood swim team suit. "Remember last year I told you I swam at Tilden Woods Community Pool in Rockville."

Veronica was sitting on a wooden bench in front of her locker. She looked up at Terri, nodding and appraising.

The first event at practice was the four hundred meters individual medley. Terri started off even with Veronica in the butterfly, both in the lead, but then in the backstroke, she gained a body length. And on to the breaststroke, Terri increased her lead to three body lengths. And then came the freestyle, Terri's strongest event.

After the turn, she began ripping through the water with powerful strokes and kicks, all in perfect unison. When she came to the finish line, Veronica was in second with still half the pool length to go.

As the girls stayed in the pool catching their breath, the swim team coach was clapping his hands and hooting out his pleasure at his new wunderkind. "Terri, where have you been all my life?"

Terri also finished first in the individual backstroke and freestyle, where again she dominated. After that first day of practice, Veronica had been distant from Terri as they dressed in the locker room. There had been something of the ice maiden in her aloofness as she slipped into her flip-flops as though Terri were not there.

But over the course of the first week of practice, Veronica began to initiate a closer friendship with Terri: making a point to talk with her before and after practice, eating lunch with her at school, and always greeting her when they passed in the school hallways.

"After school, let's study together in the library for finals," Veronica suggested at lunch.

Rather seamlessly, over the course of the summer after seventh grade, Veronica pulled Terri into her best friend orbit. Terri thought maybe it was because she had never held her swimming exploits over Veronica or the other girls on the team, as she had deflected any praise from the coach or the other swimmers with a *no-big-deal* smile.

After Kenwood's swim season, Terri had her first sleepover at Veronica's house.

"May I ask a personal question, Veronica?"

"Sure," Veronica said. "Fire away."

"Why did you change your name from Gretchen to Veronica?"

"Gretchen is such a frumpy name and *sooo* old-world German. On my twelfth birthday, my father told me that my middle name was after my great-grandmother, Countess Veronica Von Claussen, with two *S*s."

They were under the covers of Veronica's bed, facing each other. Each girl had an elbow cocked and chin propped in the palm of her hand.

"I never liked the name Gretchen, and for some reason, that clinched it for me."

"Wasn't it hard to get your parents and grade-school friends to change after calling you Gretchen for all your life?"

Veronica rolled over on her back, with her fingers laced behind her neck. "I wouldn't answer to Gretchen." She reached over to the lamp on her nightstand and turned it off. The room became pitch-black. "Eventually they accepted me as Veronica—even my parents."

Lying there in the darkness and in the silence of the room, Terri felt as though some unknowable knowledge had passed between them.

Unknowable and blunt, Terri thought. Veronica never seemed to grasp the impact of her words. She could have been gentler.

"Matt and I made love. I'm so sorry."

Or "I slept with Matt. Can you ever forgive me?"

But that was never Veronica's way.

"I fucked Matt."

Fucked? What a horrible word. And not only did she f ... Matt, but she fucked me in the process, Terri thought, letting the horrible word explode in her mind.

Terri liked the way Kevin had handled things back at the campground: few words but understanding words.

She rode past the Bethany Beach water tower, indicating less than two miles back to the house. Finally Terri eased up on the pedals. She hadn't realized how hard she had been pedaling until she stopped at the traffic light at Fred Hudson Road before continuing when the light turned green.

At another red light at Garfield Parkway, Terri glanced at the totem pole. In the dusky light, she couldn't make out the details, but in her mind's eye, she saw the Indian's shuttered eyes with the etched tears. Never had she imagined them sadder.

As she came down her street, the sun, now an orange ball, was sinking toward the red-streaked horizon tottering below a bruised purple sky. *How heartbreakingly beautiful.*

By the time Terri secured her bike in the backyard at the bike rack, her mind had eased some from the exercise of riding five miles into the wind, but still she felt a bit unhinged, as though she were in some other reality. She found her mother in the kitchen, cleaning dishes at the sink.

"Hi, honey," her mother said as she turned and offered a welcoming smile to her daughter.

Terri sat on a barstool at the kitchen hatch. Terri looked at her father's empty easy chair. "Where's Dad?"

"After dinner, Irv Hudson came by, and they went to the VFW." Betty Landers put her hands on the bar counter and studied her daughter for a moment. "Are you hungry?"

"No thanks, Mom," Terri said in a sad little voice.

"Anything you want to talk about?"

Terri could never hide her feelings from her mother, who could always read her like a book. But the sympathetic tone in Betty's voice broke something loose inside of Terri as she felt a swell of emotion in her throat. "People, Mom. Not who I thought they were."

"Matt?" Her mother said ever so softly.

Terri lifted her brow and made a *sorta* face.

"I once dated a dangerously handsome young man back in Chicago before I knew your father."

Terri leaned back in her stool, her eyes saying, *Please continue.*

"It was a couple of years after the war, and I was working as a receptionist for a law firm. This dashingly handsome young man in a three-piece suit was standing in front of my desk. He seemed to have appeared out of nowhere."

Betty wiped her hands on a dish rag, came around, and took a seat next to her daughter. "Next thing I know we were dating, and oh, was it something. We went to fine restaurants, shows, and grand parties."

For the first time, Terri felt as though she and her mother were women talking, not as mother and daughter, but woman to woman. "What was his name, Mom?"

"Eddie Reynolds," Betty said with a remembering look right at her daughter.

Terri's mother was a slender brunette with bright blue eyes, a well-formed nose, and a delicate chin. Betty Landers was a quiet, reserved woman, whom Terri had never once seen let her hair down. She had never come close to drunkenness, and she was always polite and caring. In Terri's eyes she was the perfect mother—well, almost. She was a bit too inquiring at times, though Terri knew that she would be the same.

"What happened, Mom?"

"Loretta Sullivan—my best friend who was a real looker—happened." Betty shrugged. "It was all for the better, though painful at the time to find out my best friend was not who I thought she was. And the fella I had fallen head over heels for shared the same boat."

In the rescue of a life
Comes the wisdom
Of our days
That we are but
A small speck
In the eternal haze

Terri woke early and went out to the porch with the Lincoln biography. The sky was pale blue in the dawn light, and in her mind's eye, she saw a glowing orange sun inching its way up the ocean's horizon. It was going to be a hot day, as she could already feel the humidity beginning to build.

She opened the book to a chapter titled "The Gathering Storm." She had tried to read it last night in bed, but yesterday's events kept ricocheting in her mind. It had been such a wonderful time at Whiskey Beach with Black Bart, his Rally Crew, and their offbeat patriotism as well as the different groups of kids partying with a joyful vigor and being in the company of Kevin.

Then it was on to the Bottle and Cork, the raucous crowd, the wet T-shirt contest with Joe Bock and Porn Girl, and of course Black Bart coming to Terri's rescue before it all came crashing down with Veronica stating in such a cold and uncaring tone, "The fortress was breached. I fucked Matt."

Wow! Total betrayal. Part of Terri wanted nothing to do with Veronica, but that would be impossible since she still had the rest of the summer to work with her. She wasn't sure how she would handle it.

The boisterous throaty chirps of the purple martins drew Terri's attention to the birdhouse. The birds were coming and going in a rush of activity, ducking into the entrance holes and exiting. It seemed as though choreographed, and it seemed a wonder they didn't collide. There must have been fifty of them.

The birds' chirps grew louder and with a calamitous tremor. Terri stood for a closer look. The black snake was caught in the wire mesh that she had installed at the base of the pole.

As she neared the snake, Terri got a whiff of a musky pungent odor that grew stronger as she stood a few feet from the wiggling, trapped reptile in a ball of mesh wire.

"Trying to breach my fortress, you slithering black devil," Terri said aloud.

She had told Greg about her previous encounter with the snake, and he had told her that it sounded like a black rat snake that was not venomous but could bite if threatened.

"So be careful with them," he had warned.

Terri had two choices: let the creature stay entangled and die a slow, painful death or somehow untangle it, setting it free. She could wake her father, who growing up in rural Kansas must have had experience with this type of situation, but she decided against bothering him.

Handle it yourself, Terri thought as she went out to the shed and removed the rake, a garden hoe, and a pair of rubber gloves.

"Need help?"

Terri turned and saw her father's friend from the VFW approaching. "Mr. Hudson?"

"I found your father's wallet in my car and left it on the porch when I saw you. Looks like you could use a hand from an old Sussex County country boy."

Irv Hudson was of average height but solidly built with a shock of steel-gray hair atop a monumental head and a wide and high forehead. His smooth face was unlined, but his eyes had the look of someone who had been through difficult times. Her father told Terri that Irv had served under General Patton in the war as a teenager, fighting the Germans at an age younger than Terri was now.

"Thank you, yes. This snake keeps trying to get at the martin house." Terri shrugged and offered a hand to her wire trap.

Irv eyed her preventive measure and nodded. "That's not bad. Stopped it pretty good. Of course, it is its nature." He gave Terri a knowing lift of his brow. "A snake being a snake." Irv placed his foot gently on the back of the head of the snake that didn't move. "It appears pretty tuckered out." He removed a pocketknife from the front pocket of his trousers and began cutting through the tangled mesh.

"Do you want these gloves, Mr. Hudson?"

"No need," he said.

Within a minute, Irv held the freed snake firmly in his grip, his large right hand under the head and his thumb at the back. "If you could get me a large paper bag, I will take it for a long drive and release it where it can do no further harm to the martins."

Terri returned with a grocery bag. Irv placed the viper in the bag, tail first, and removed his hand quickly while with the other hand squeezed it shut.

Irv smiled a *no-problem* smile. "So," he said, "the martins are now safe, and I will let this snake go back to being a snake."

On her bike ride over to the pool, Terri had a sudden rush of guilt that she had left Greg alone to fix the chlorine problem. Also adding to her guilt was the fact that all day yesterday she hadn't once thought about the pool, Greg, or that horrible inspector.

When she arrived at the pool, she saw Greg's car in the parking lot. She found Greg on the pool deck vacuuming the shallow end, his back to her.

"Morning, Greg."

Greg turned and smiled a hello.

"Pool open?" Terri asked as she took the vacuum from Greg.

"After I made the repair, the head of the board called the head of the Health Department, and the pool was back open at noon. Billy and I guarded. I called you and Veronica a couple of times." He grabbed the leaf skimmer leaning against the guard stand and extended it into the pool, gathering a few random leaves. "But never got an answer."

"Sorry," Terri said.

"No problem." He stopped netting and looked at Terri. "Do anything fun yesterday?"

"Hi," Veronica said, approaching and taking the leaf skimmer from Greg. "I saw Billy in the guard room. He told me about yesterday."

Greg laughed. "While Billy and I held down the fort, I bet you two had a time for yourselves." Without waiting for an answer, he then headed over toward the guard room, leaving the two girls standing alone.

Terri concentrated on moving the vacuum along the pool bottom, waiting for Veronica's next move.

"Do you hate me?" Veronica asked in a soft yet matter-of-fact voice without a trace of shame.

"Why Matt? Why me?" Terri stopped vacuuming and then turned back and faced Veronica.

"I wish I had never done it. That I had saved myself for Josh." Veronica removed the leaf skimmer from the water and banged a few wayward leaves into a trash can.

"You didn't answer my question, Veronica," Terri said in a raised voice.

"Hey, Terri."

Terri looked over toward the clubhouse and saw Billy.

"Greg asked if you could backwash before opening."

By noon, "Marco … Polo" was a constant refrain. The pool was teeming with energized kids and a few wading adults watching the kids. Most of the adults were lounging poolside, some were playing cards at tables, and others gathered in a circle, immersed in happy talk. Terri was on duty at the lower section of the pool; Veronica was at the T-section, guarding the deep end.

Terri was in a funk. She wanted to finish it out with Veronica, but would most likely have to wait until after closing. She blew her whistle at a boy splashing with too much zeal.

"Hey, no more." she shouted at him.

The boy looked up at Terri with a *what-me* look. Terri lifted her brow. *Yes, you.*

She felt like lifting her brow to Veronica, who suddenly jumped down from her guard chair and dove in the deep end.

Terri stood up and saw Veronica emerge from the water with a little girl, no more than seven. Terri jumped down from the guard chair and raced over as Veronica towed the child to the pool's edge. Terri bent down and lifted the seemingly lifeless body out of the water and placed her on her back on the pool deck.

As crowd gathered around, a woman shrieked, "Oh my God! It's my baby girl. Oh my God!"

Terri said to Veronica in a raised voice, "Run to the guard room and tell Greg to call for an ambulance."

Terri placed her ear next to the girl's mouth to see if she was breathing. Nothing. She checked the girl's pulse on her neck. Nothing. As Terri opened the girl's mouth, everything grew quiet. She no longer heard the hubbub of people gathering around or the sobbing mother. She pinched the nose and breathed three times into the girl's tiny mouth and then applied pressure to her bony chest, one hand atop the other. Back to the mouth … back to applying pressure. She continued for what seemed an eternity before the girl coughed up water.

"Nice work," said a strong male voice that brought Terri back to whatever state she had entered.

Officer Jim Brewer bent over and brought the coughing girl to a sitting position, tapping her gently on the back. As she continued to cough, droplets of water emerged from her mouth.

"Mommy," the little girl said in a weak, pleading voice.

"I'm here, honey." The mother was on her knees next to Officer Brewer.

"Clear the way!"

Two rescue squad paramedics, dressed in dark blue uniforms with American flag patches on their short sleeves, were wheeling a gurney up the pool deck. The lead paramedic ran ahead and checked over the little girl, examining her eyes, checking her pulse, and checking her over completely.

"Is she okay?" the mother asked.

"She appears to be fine," the paramedic said. "But we are going to take her to the hospital to be safe."

The paramedic then lifted the little girl up on the gurney, and with the mother holding her daughter's hand, he wheeled her away. Terri stood and felt her knees shake as a trembling sensation shot down her spine.

"You saved that girl's life," a man said to Terri.

"She's a hero," a woman affirmed.

Terri grabbed Officer Brewer's forearm to steady herself.

"Let's get you seated for a minute," Jim Brewer said.

People started clapping as Officer Brewer guided Terri to a chair under the shade of an umbrella. After a couple of minutes, Terri felt fine, but not before she received congratulations from folks and Greg checking on her.

"I'm fine." She smiled at Greg. "I guess this makes up for missing work yesterday."

By late afternoon, only a few people remained at the pool. Billy was in the guard chair at the deep end as a man swam laps.

Terri started at the shallow end, straightening chairs and taking down umbrellas. Veronica was doing the same at the deep end. Terri had not spoken with Veronica since the rescue of the little girl, whom Greg said had been released from the hospital, good as new.

Terri had taken the CPR class the spring of senior year of high school, along with Veronica and six adults. It was the first time CPR had been offered at the YMCA in Bethesda, and Terri's father suggested she take it since she had just received her lifeguard certificate.

"You just may save a life someday," her father said.

Terri remembered the CPR instructor's words. "In a crisis situation, a steady hand and steady nerves are critical in the saving of a life. And remember: push hard and fast."

In that surreal moment of bringing that little girl's body back to life, Terri never thought about her nerves. She was too concerned with counting her breaths and then the firm compressions on little girl's chest. How tiny and vulnerable that lifeless body seemed. How peaceful she looked, her eyes closed as though dreaming some faraway dream before she coughed up water and the eyes peeked open with a frightened look that asked, *Where am I?*

The saving of a life had brought into focus for Terri how trivial her concern about Matt and Veronica's tryst now seemed. She, Terri Landers, had saved a life that might go on to live another eighty or ninety years, well into the twenty-first century. As she clicked down an umbrella, it dawned on Terri that, if Veronica had not acted quickly by spotting the little girl and going in the water and pulling her out, that little girl would be dead, unable to live out her life. Yes, Terri had performed CPR, but it had been a team effort.

Terri worked her way up to the deep end. Veronica was one table over, trying to get a difficult umbrella down.

"Let me help." Terri pushed hard on the metal ring above the clip and eased the resistant canopy down.

"Thanks," Veronica said.

"Can we walk our bikes home and talk?" Terri asked.

**In the aftermath
The truth arrives at my door,
An inexorable realization:
She is nevermore**

Terri and Veronica walked their bikes down Half Moon Circle side by side. Terri hoped that Veronica would initiate conversation, but deep down she realized it would have to be her.

"Did you hear," Terri asked, "that Greg called the hospital and the little girl is fine?"

"Un huh," Veronica said as though half-listening.

"Veronica," Terri said sharply as she stopped walking. "What is it with you?"

Veronica had walked ahead. She stopped and waited for Terri to come up to her. "I ..." Veronica moved off the road to a side lawn as cars came in both directions. "I didn't mean to hurt you, Terri. I had too much to drink, and *it* just happened."

"You didn't hurt me, Veronica." Terri moved her bike off onto the grass and kicked out the kickstand, freeing her hands, which she threw in front of herself. "You disappointed me. I thought we were best friends."

Veronica started rolling her bike down the road, her back to Terri.

"That's it," Terri said. "Walk away like it never happened."

Veronica stopped and turned her head over her shoulder. "It's just not that big a deal." She shrugged. "Matt didn't mean anything to me or you for that matter." Veronica lifted her chin to indicate one more thing. "We saved a life today. That seems a whole lot more important."

She made a face, *Right?*

True, Terri thought, but still it was wrong what Veronica had done.

"Why can't you just say how sorry you are?"

"Look," Veronica said in an abrupt voice, "if it had been someone like Kevin, who obviously means something to you—well, I would have never done that—but if I had, I would be truly sorry, but Matt was a mistake we both made."

At dinner with her parents, Terri filled them in on saving a life at the pool.

"Wow," her father said, "our little girl is a hero."

"Veronica too," Terri added in a grudging, slightly vexed tone.

Betty slid a look across the table at her daughter and smiled understandingly. It was a private smile between mother and daughter, a grin of reassurance. And in that quicksilver moment, something passed between them, something that indicated Betty understood exactly what Terri was experiencing, for she had been there herself all those years ago.

After dinner, Terri received a phone call from Kevin, wanting to know if she wanted to watch the fireworks tomorrow, the Fourth of July, on the beach in Bethany.

"Josh and Veronica are going," he said.

"Ah ... okay," Terri said.

"Problem?" Kevin said. "Veronica, right? You are gathering angry momentum toward her in regard to her dalliance with Matt."

Terri didn't want to admit to Kevin that Matt was that important to her, especially since he wasn't. But then why was she so upset?

"No, it's just ... well ... yeah sure, I *want* to go with you, and if Josh and Veronica have to be included, that's fine."

They agreed to meet at the sub shop and then find a good spot on the beach before the fireworks. After hanging up the phone, a wave of fatigue came over Terri. It had been a long couple of days in her life. But she wanted to finish the Lincoln biography.

She learned that Lincoln had lost two sons at young ages. Had she read this previously and forgotten such an important fact? One son, Eddie, was not even three when he passed, and Willie, born eleven months after his brother's death, died before his twelfth birthday. How unimaginable the loss of two sons.

Was Veronica right? Was she making too big a deal out of her and

Matt, who had moved on to Brittany as though he hadn't missed a beat? And were there other girls he had been with behind her back?

Terri wondered if she had been Veronica's friend all these years because being associated with a beautiful girl like her was a status symbol. Like dating Matt? But she had enjoyed more than that. Veronica's offbeat outlook on things and even her mocking assessment of people, except when it had hit so close to home.

"Malice toward none," Lincoln said in his second inauguration speech, one month before his assassination.

Malice no, but a strong distrust and possibly a growing dislike for those two beautiful creatures, Terri thought as she opened the last chapter titled "The Final Days."

When love is subtle
Do not look the other way
For it may never return
In a life now splayed

Monday, July 4, was another busy day at the pool with all four guards in attendance. Terri and Veronica had greeted each other on the pool deck before opening, exchanging guarded good mornings. Once the pool opened, they kept a distance, not in proximity but in lack of talking. Normally when both or one wasn't on guard duty, they would converse, if only for a minute or two, as though reaffirming their friendship. It was small talk, mostly about the upcoming school year, plans for the evening, or anything that struck their fancy.

But since Veronica told of *the thing with Matt*, they tacitly had given each other space. At noon, Terri went to the guard room to eat her lunch. Veronica was sitting at the desk, pulling out an apple, a small bag of chips, and a sandwich wrapped in a baggie.

"Hi," Terri said in a flat tone as she removed her lunch from the cabinet.

Veronica looked at Terri, her eyes saying, *Are we good?* She offered half her sandwich to Terri, who took a seat at the table.

"No thanks," Terri replied. "I'm tired of peanut butter and jelly."

Veronica shrugged. *No biggie.*

"I'm going to let Josh have his way with me tonight," Veronica said.

Terri nearly gagged on a mouthful of ham and cheese on rye. "What?"

"We talked after the Bottle and Cork when he drove me home."

Terri put down her sandwich, with her eyes on Veronica.

"I told him about Matt. Everything."

"And?"

"I told him it meant nothing and I wished I had saved myself for him." Veronica made a face. *I did it.*

Terri, with Matt and Veronica's tryst still in her craw, had told herself not to encourage conversation with Veronica, but her curiosity got the best of her.

"Well?" she said. "What did Josh say?"

"He appreciated my honesty and said that it was better to never be number one because statistically it usually ends in a permanent breakup."

"Let me guess," Terri said as she leaned back in her chair. "He proposed that you allow him the honor of being number two."

"Yes," Veronica said as she took a bite into her peanut-butter-and-jelly sandwich. "And"—she paused as she took a swig from her can of Coke, washing down her food before continuing—"you should consider Kevin as being the exception to the rule."

When Terri got home from the pool, she found her mother in the kitchen at the stove stirring a pot of spaghetti sauce and meatballs, a recipe passed down from her mother-in-law. The house wafted in the sweet aroma of tomato and herbs.

"Need help, Mom?" Terri asked, standing at the bar, peering across the kitchen hatch.

"I have it under control," Betty said as she gave a subtle, yet inquiring, lift of her brow, as though to transpose her declarative statement into a question.

Her mother turned the heat to low and covered the pot with a lid. She stepped to her left and lifted a kitchen towel off the countertop. As she wiped her hands, she made a little face, indicating, *One more thing.*

"As you can see, I am making your favorite."

Terri paused to sniff the mouthwatering aroma of homemade tomato sauce and meatballs stuffed with mozzarella cheese. "I should have told you earlier, Mom. Veronica and I are going to the Yellow Submarine for subs."

When Terri was younger, her mother would oftentimes make spaghetti sauce and meatballs for dinner the night before a big swim meet. "Your father says carbohydrates and protein help with endurance," her mother used to say.

"Just the two of you?" her mother asked, as though she knew there were others involved.

"Kevin and his roommate from college are meeting us."

"Kevin McGregor from last summer?" Her mother drew out his surname with a trace of a lilt, Mc … Greg … or. She placed her hands on the countertop and leaned forward, her eyes searching her daughter's.

Terri nodded. "Yes, Mom," she said in a tone hinting aggravation. They were back to mother-and-daughter relationship.

Her mother smiled, her expression that of approval. "I always liked that boy."

Inside her bedroom, Terri decided she wanted to look nice for Kevin, something special. She opened her closet and spotted her flowery smock shirt, which she had ironed.

Oh yes, she thought as she removed it from its hanger. *Now is the time to wear it. My flower-girl shirt.*

She looked in the mirror. Her golden tan contrasted perfectly with the ivory-colored shirt and embroidered bright flowers. Never before had she felt that way, dressing specifically to impress a certain guy. Not Kevin last year. Not Matt. Not the boys she went out with in high school or college.

She noticed the Scottish terrier figurine on her dresser; its little circles for eyes appeared to be looking at her, as though to say, *I'm here with you.* She remembered her words to Kevin at the Spill the Milk booth when he had asked what prize she wanted.

"I'll have the Scotty."

She would take the figurine with her to school.

Terri ran a brush through her thick hair, hair that her mother said she had inherited from her grandmother, her mother's mother. "A mane of dark brown luxury" was an expression her mother used to say when she would brush Terri's hair before bed.

When she was younger and her hair longer, her mother taught her how to put her hair in a french braid. How patient her mother had been teaching ten-year-old Terri the complicated process of separating her hair in three sections and then transferring one section over the other, adding hair to one section and then another.

But when Terri got involved in competitive swimming, it was easier to tuck shorter hair under her swim cap, and it was easier all around to maintain shorter hair. On occasion she had braided her shorter version, and though she always received compliments, it wasn't worth the hassle. It had been years since she last braided. Ah, but for tonight she decided to make an exception.

When she finished sectioning and twisting her hair into a single braid, she was more than a little taken by her appearance. It was though a curtain had been pulled. Her young, creamy-smooth face was suddenly striking. Her eyebrows arched in perfect symmetry. Her high cheekbones, no longer in the cover and shadow of hair, were flushed with color, sweeping down to a strong yet feminine chin that anchored the new her.

"Oh, Terri," her mother exclaimed when she got a look at her daughter. "You look beautiful."

Her father then came in the backdoor off the kitchen from the backyard. "Ready for a cocktail, Betty?"

"Richard," Terri's mother said, "take a good look at your daughter."

"What's that, Betty?"

Betty directed her husband into the living room, where Terri was hoping to make a clean getaway without further inquiry about her evening.

Her father stopped in his tracks when he got a look at Terri. "Oh," he said in a tone of surprise. He moved closer to Terri, his eyes appraising. "Is this our little girl? You look beautiful, honey."

This was high praise coming from a quiet, taciturn man, a man who Terri always knew was silently proud of her. She knew the way he used to nod his approval when after swim meets she would set another county record or make honor roll in school. Richard Landers's face showed his pride, but rarely did he speak it.

A man who had lived through the Great Depression and World War II had always kept his emotions in reserve as though not to jinx. But something seemed to have broken loose for a moment, as Richard beamed a huge smile upon Terri.

As the smile faded, he nodded and said, "Going out, are you?" He put that out there more as a statement of fact. "Have yourself a grand time tonight."

On the bike ride over to Veronica's house, Terri considered Veronica's advice in regard to Kevin but was more than a little uncertain. She thought there was something special with him, but didn't want to rush into anything yet.

She would rather see how things developed over the course of the school year, with their schools only a two-hour drive apart. Of course that was what Kevin had in mind last year until Terri put the kibosh on it. She assumed he would be agreeable to seeing each other during next semester, but at this point, she was taking nothing for granted.

Last year, she considered him not quite attractive enough, not quite studly enough to spend more time with. She thought their time together had run its course. But after dating the epitome of studly in Matt, Terri was seeing Kevin in an entirely new light.

Patriotic lights in the night
Illuminate the truth
Mr. Right is there before you
As living proof

Terri and Veronica approached Kevin and Josh at the back of a line forming outside the door of the Yellow Submarine that was crammed with people.

Kevin smiled at Terri and nodded appreciatively at the smock shirt. He leaned toward her and said softly, "The return of my flower girl. Nice."

"This line is something else," Josh said as general conversation.

"I have an idea," Kevin suggested. "Is there a pay phone nearby?"

"On the corner of Atlantic and Garfield." Terri pointed across the street.

"I'll phone in four steak-and-cheese subs." Kevin made a face seeking approval.

"Go for it," Terri said.

Kevin nodded an *okay* and made a beeline for the pay phone. Ten minutes later, Kevin walked out of the sub shop clutching in one hand two bags containing subs and fries, and in the other, he underhand balanced a takeout carrier cradling four Styrofoam cups, with lids secured, of Cokes packed in ice.

"Good job, Kev," Josh said as he took the soft carrier from him.

"Let's eat on the beach." Veronica lifted a beach bag. "I packed a blanket."

Rolling waves crashed on the shore, momentarily drowning out the hum of activity on the boardwalk in measured intervals. Veronica and Terri spread the blanket on the edge of the soft, cool sand near the ocean.

The blanket was made of lightweight terrycloth with flat woven gray-and-white stripes. It felt luxurious, and Terri wondered if Veronica had purchased it for her night of romance with Josh.

Terri was famished, and the steak and cheese was steaming hot and deliciously greasy. She wasn't sure if it was the setting with the salty air and gentle breeze adding something to the experience. Or was it the fact that she was with Kevin, even though it included Veronica, whose presence was impossible to ignore? But she didn't want anything to get in the way of her evening with Kevin.

On the bike ride into town, Terri had tried to convince herself that Veronica had gone through a transformation, a developmental phase, and that she was no longer the person who had done the deed with Matt. But she failed miserably at it. She would have never ever done that to Veronica. Yes, Matt was no longer an issue, but Veronica was.

"Where are we watching the fireworks?" Josh asked. He was sitting on Veronica's left. Terri was on her right, and Kevin was on the other end of the blanket.

"Let's go up to Fifth Street," Veronica said, glancing at Terri.

"Okay with me," Terri said.

She looked at Kevin. *What do you think?*

"Sure, it won't be as crowded, and we can get a front-row seat."

After eating, they decided to walk the beach up to Fifth Street. It was still light out. Though diminished, a washed-out blue sky with an apron of tawny yellow skirting the horizon provided a backdrop to the moon.

Terri and Veronica removed their flip-flops and walked barefoot along the shoreline, leaving their footprints in the wet sand before the water came and washed them away.

There were only a few people on Fifth Street beach, a group of college-aged kids on a blanket and two middle-aged couples in beach chairs, all sitting near the water.

"Let's go down a little farther," Veronica said, throwing her hand over her shoulder with her finger pointing forward. She was like a hunter in search of the perfect blind.

They stopped at a sign indicating private beach.

"This is good," Veronica said.

"It's like no-man's land." Josh offered a hand toward the private beach, where farther down, murmurs of laughter and happy talk were barely audible. He then offered a hand back toward Fifth Street, where people were barely visible in the dusky light.

"Our own private viewing," Kevin said.

The girls spread out the blanket. They sat in a row as before: boy, girl, girl, boy. They were facing the ocean, now dark and shadowy. The horizon was a dying yellow, and the moon was a ghostly white orb, floating in the darkening sky.

At dark, the sky lit up in an array of whistling Roman candles, exploding sky rockets bursting into splintering shards into an array of lights. Aerial shells exploded into a circle. One after another, the fireworks assaulted the sky in booms and crackles.

Terri had witnessed this display last year, but it all seemed more magnificent, more moving. She felt so in the moment.

"Wow," Josh said at the climax, as the sky seemed to explode into an eruption of earsplitting bangs and booms, casting a rainbow of colors across the ocean. "All we need is the *1812 Overture*," he shouted over the ruckus in the sky.

The display ended with one last crackling pop of a Roman candle, lighting up the sky momentarily before fading to black.

Kevin reached for Terri's hand and whispered in her ear, "It was special this year."

Terri turned to him. "I was thinking the same thing."

"Let's walk and talk," Kevin suggested. "Just the two of us."

"We're going to leave you two to your own devices," Kevin said to Veronica and Josh. He then stood and offered his hand to Terri.

"Let's meet back at the boardwalk at eleven," Veronica suggested.

"Eleven thirty," Josh said. "Don't want to rush this evening." He leaned into Veronica, both still sitting, and kissed her on the lips with arms around backs, as they fell down in a lying position, face-to-face, lost in their own world.

Kevin and Terri walked onto the private beach, which was now empty. The moon was significantly higher in the sky. The light it threw across the water had an amber glow, like a welcoming oceanic doormat.

"So quiet after all that bombast earlier," Kevin said as he came to a halt. He turned to Terri and took both her hands in his. "By the way, my flower girl, you look absolutely beautiful tonight."

Terri came up to him, her body against his, her chest against his, her face in his. Kevin started to speak, and Terri silenced him with a finger on his lip. He wrapped an arm around her waist and kissed her, his lips soft and warm. He smelled boyishly fresh. They went down into the sand, tongues finding tongues, the heat rising in Terri's neck and spreading like wildfire down her torso. Kevin slid his hand under the flower shirt, underneath her bra, rubbing her breast.

"Kevin?" Terri panted.

Kevin's other hand was now on the other breast.

"Kevin?" she repeated.

Kevin drew back, his true-blue eyes fixed on hers. "Yes," he said as he seemed to come back from lustful boy to good-guy Kevin.

"I want to wait."

Kevin took a deep breath as though collecting himself. "For Mr. Right?"

Terri smiled and then laughed softly. "No," she said in a mock scolding tone. She leaned her head forward and kissed Kevin on the cheek. "I've already found him."

Time is elusive
As a hummingbird's wings
Thwarting your memory
But not the essence of things

BETHANY BEACH 2017

Bethany West had not changed all that much in the last forty years, though a good number of the homes had been renovated with expanded living areas, additional bedrooms, and updated kitchens, but the neighborhood still maintained that all-American appeal of a simpler time. And the trees, which were so few and tiny when first Terri came here, provided a welcome shade in the summer months.

It was early morning, and Terri sat on the side porch in her robe with a cup of green tea in hand. It was the calm before the storm. In the closet, she had hanging a shirt that she had taken special care of and worn every Fourth of July since all those years back. She remembered almost wearing the flower-girl shirt to the Bottle and Cork, the time Veronica had told Terri of her romp with Matt, but she had an intuition that it wasn't the right time.

Had fate somehow played a hand in her not wearing it that day? To save it for the right moment, the day of the Fourth right here in Bethany Beach when she realized that Kevin was the one.

The Fourth was definitely a special day for Terri's family. Kevin Jr. and Anna would be arriving later today with the twins, Sara and Jenn, who were born on the Fourth of July five years ago.

How appropriate, Terri thought. *We get to celebrate it here in this beach house with so many fond memories.*

The foundation of those memories began when Terri and Kevin had continued dating at the start of their junior year, and by the spring of senior year, it seemed a done deal.

"After we graduate and find jobs, let's rent an apartment together back home at Parkside," Kevin had suggested on a Sunday-morning walk in a park near Terri's campus.

Terri came to a halt along the edge of a creek, its current strong from the spring melt. "To see if we're compatible over a long stretch?" she asked as she glanced up at splintering sunlight emerging through the green canopy.

"No," Kevin said, "so that you are sure I *am* Mr. Right." He tossed a stone in the creek and looked off for a moment and then back at Terri. "I knew from the first moment we met on the beach at Bethany that you were the one for me."

After three months together at Parkside, Terri told Kevin that she wanted to get married. "If you're willing."

By this time, both had good jobs. Kevin had recently completed training as a loan officer for a mortgage company in Bethesda, and Terri, who had switched majors and graduated with an environmental science degree, was employed by an environmental firm in Rockville.

Of course, Kevin was willing, and in June 1980, they were married. Two years later Kevin Jr. was born.

Terri left her job after less than a year, spending her first year of motherhood as a stay-at-home mom, during which time she obtained her real estate license, allowing more flexibility in regard to spending time with her son, who went to day care three days a week.

When Kevin Jr. entered kindergarten, Terri returned to working full-time at the environmental firm, and that same year, she and Kevin purchased a house in North Chevy Chase Village, an incorporated community of older homes and tree-lined streets.

Over the years, Terri and Kevin had invested wisely and saved a nice pile of money, and five years ago she decided to retire. Terri filled her time doing volunteer work for the Red Cross and watching the grandkids. She loved her time with Sara and Jenn, such lovely girls, though a bit rambunctious, which became an asset when Kevin had finally agreed to a remodel of the beach house.

"We need another bedroom and more space for Sara and Jenn," Kevin said to Terri after the one-year-old twins and their parents had stayed for a cramped and noisy week.

Terri worked with an architect and had plans drawn for a remodel of the beach house her parents had purchased that unforgettable summer of 1977. The work was completed three years ago, and the extra space with a spanking new and bigger kitchen and an additional bedroom, plus an expansion of the living room and porch, made things more comfortable when the house was alive with three generations of McGregors.

Oh, how Terri wished her parents could have lived to see their great-grandchildren. Her dad had died from a stroke ten years ago, and her mother passed seven years ago from renal failure. But after her father retired in 1990, both spent a good deal of their time in Bethany Beach, especially in the summer. Her father was always more relaxed in Bethany Beach, and retirement brought a whole new side to Terri's father, a carpe diem side.

Richard Landers bought himself a used MG convertible that he had spent a year restoring and then kept it in Bethany Beach to tool around in. He and Irv Hudson, who became very close with Richard after both had retired, would go off on fishing trips in Irv's RV down the East Coast, all the way to Florida in the winter.

Betty also got into the swing of things in Bethany, joining a women's club, doing volunteer work, and in the summer relaxing on Third Street beach with a group of Bethany West neighbors.

But Betty and Richard never considered living full-time in Bethany Beach, especially after Kevin Jr. was born. Being a grandfather was the beginning of Richard's transformation from going-through-the-motions life to actually looking forward to spending time with his grandson: fishing on Saturdays down on the Potomac River, attending Little League baseball games, and having Kevin Jr. and his parents down to Bethany for two weeks every summer. He was a doting, if still reticent, Grandman, a name that Kevin Jr. had assigned to him as a toddler.

It seemed a blessing to Terri, even though she lost her parents at relatively young ages. Both passed in their eighty-second year. Both went quickly. Her dad died two days after the debilitating stroke that left him bedridden and speechless; her mother went into the hospital to combat a viral infection, and one week later, her kidneys gave out.

From time to time, when alone on the porch, Terri would think back to the summer of 1977 when the direction of her life changed, as did the lives of those in her life. Back at their respective colleges, Kevin and Terri didn't see each other every weekend, but when Kevin's work schedule had an open weekend, he would make the two-hour drive to Terri's campus. It made their time together more special.

Veronica and Josh's true-blue romance fell apart after their summer together. The distance from their schools—more than five hundred miles—and Veronica falling for one of her professors ended it. But not before Josh had his way with Veronica on a "night of glorious, lustful sex on the beach," as Veronica described it to Terri the following day at the pool.

Veronica's life took a sudden change during spring break of her junior year of college when a modeling talent scout spotted her in Daytona Beach. Terri received a call from Veronica in Los Angeles, telling her that she had signed a contract with a modeling agency. Terri never saw her again. She invited Veronica to her wedding, but she had a modeling gig in Milan.

Over the years, the calls from Veronica became fewer and further apart until there were no more. Veronica never appeared at any of the Walter Johnson class reunions, and Terri hadn't heard from her in over twenty years. Up to that point Veronica had not married.

She had considered contacting Veronica's parents but decided against it, an intuitive sense that a reunion would not be a good thing. It had never been the same after the summer of 1977.

Reflecting back, there had been a sense of emptiness hovering over Veronica, as though her heart was never quite in it, whether it be romance, friendships, or her outlook on each day.

Terri remembered a day at the pool when she had commented to Veronica, "Sometimes the sky is so beautifully blue it makes me so happy to be alive. Do you know what I mean?"

She leaned back in the lifeguard chair and looked down at her friend, who was cleaning up debris on the pool deck from the previous night's storm.

Veronica paused from collecting leaves with a leaf skimmer and scanned the pool as children sat on the copingstones, anxiously eyeing the big circular clock at the clubhouse, waiting for the adult swim to end.

"I like the sky when the sun begins to sink and it turns all different shades of purple and pink as though the end of the world were near. Savor it while you can."

Never really knew that girl, Terri thought.

She turned her mind to the upcoming weekend. Soon the twins and Kevin Jr. and Anna would arrive, and once again the house would be teeming with three generations of McGregors.

She saw a bike rider turn the corner, coming down the street. *Is that him?* Terri thought.

"It *is* Kevin," she said.

For there he came.

Printed in the United States
By Bookmasters